Advance Praise for *Chrysalis*

"This genre-bending collection defies expectations and brims with danger, desire, and the pleasures of storytelling. Anuja Varghese's surreal stories will take you places you'll never expect."
— Saleema Nawaz, author of *Songs for the End of the World*

"Anuja Varghese's stories are cheekily feminist and textured, her characters unapologetically monstrous and ordinary. I loved how many of the stories begin with deceptive quiescence and then twist into the surreal and subversive. *Chrysalis* was a joy to read!"
— Farzana Doctor, Lambda Literary Award winner and author of *Seven*

"*Chrysalis* is a provocative, taut collection, depicting women of colour who have reached the very edge of their limits. Anuja Varghese writes with surreal, urgent, sensual prose, mixing folklore and myth with the modern world. Every story is a surprise."
— Shashi Bhat, author of *The Most Precious Substance on Earth*

Chrysalis

Stories

Anuja Varghese

Published in Canada in 2023 and the USA in 2023 by House of Anansi Press Inc.
houseofanansi.com

House of Anansi Press is committed to protecting our natural environment. This book
is made of material from well-managed FSC®-certified forests, recycled materials, and
other controlled sources.

House of Anansi Press is a Global Certified Accessible™ (GCA by Benetech) publisher.
The ebook version of this book meets stringent accessibility standards and is available
to readers with print disabilities.

27 26 25 24 23   1 2 3 4 5

Library and Archives Canada Cataloguing in Publication

Title: Chrysalis : stories / Anuja Varghese.
Names: Varghese, Anuja, author.
Identifiers: Canadiana (print) 20220421013 | Canadiana (ebook) 20220421021 |
ISBN 9781487011666 (softcover) | ISBN 9781487011673 (EPUB)
Subjects: LCGFT: Short stories.
Classification: LCC PS8643.A765 C47 2023 | DDC C813/.6–dc23

Cover and book design: Alysia Shewchuk

*House of Anansi Press is grateful for the privilege to work on and create from the
Traditional Territory of many Nations, including the Anishinabeg, the Wendat, and the
Haudenosaunee, as well as the Treaty Lands of the Mississaugas of the Credit.*

With the participation of the Government of Canada
Avec la participation du gouvernement du Canada | Canadä

*We acknowledge for their financial support of our publishing program the Canada Council
for the Arts, the Ontario Arts Council, and the Government of Canada.*

Printed and bound in Canada

This book is for all the girls and women
who don't see themselves in most stories.

You are worthy of reflection,
despite what you have been told.

Content note: There are stories in this collection that contain references to self-harm, domestic violence, racism, miscarriage, homophobia, and homophobic violence.

Contents

Bhupati   1

The Vetala's Song   13

Dreams of Drowning Girls   23

In the Bone Fields   33

Remembrance   47

Milk   53

Cherry Blossom Fever   61

One, Two, Buckle My Shoe   79

Stories in the Language of the Fist   83

Night Zoo   107

Arvind   111

Chitra (Or: A Meteor Hit the Mall
     and Chitra Danced in the Flames)   119

A Cure for Fear of Screaming   147

Midnight at the Oasis   157

Chrysalis   173

Acknowledgements   191

Bhupati

The first time lightning struck Bhupati's shrine to Goddess Lakshmi, it set her face on fire. The makeshift shrine was little more than the foot-high figurine of the goddess balanced in the crumbling bird bath Maneesha had found when they moved in, overturned and filled with spiders in the patchy grass behind the rented semi. Bhupati had righted it and hosed it off, envisioning Lakshmi-Ma floating serenely on cool, clear water, surrounded by offerings of flowers and fresh fruit. But when he filled it up and placed her in, she had capsized immediately, chipping half a lotus from her third hand. He had propped her up with some loose rocks, still hopeful she could be happy, even in such a cold and brittle place as this, but soon the raccoons started arriving nightly to eat the fruit, shit in the yard, and tip over the garbage cans, and when the water froze in

November, Bhupati abandoned Lakshmi to the elements.

It was spring when the lightning struck. Bhupati was watching the storm through the sliding back doors, the rain coming down in unrelenting sheets. He could see Lakshmi out there, the red of her painted sari the only bright spot in the drenched April dusk. Maneesha was working the night shift at the hospital, leaving him to find his own dinner, which he ate standing, his fingers greasy with each fat, flaky samosa he pulled from the paper bag. It had been raining for days, alternating between freezing drizzle, brief, angry downpours, and a kind of mist with teeth. This storm though, this was the worst he had seen. On the other side of the chain-link fence separating Bhupati's yard from the Haitian family's yard, their dog made nervous circles under the overhang of the roof, barking at the electricity in the air. Maybe it was a warning.

Bhupati heard the crack before he saw the flash and behind him, the power went out in the kitchen. It went out all over Parkdale, but he didn't know that yet. All he knew for certain was that Lakshmi was burning. His first thought was to run out and save her, in what would have been an uncharacteristic act of bravery. His hand went to the door handle and he pulled, but the onslaught of weather assailed him so violently, or so he felt, that he quickly slid the door closed again. He watched the fire in the bird bath, burning in the rain. Why didn't the rain put the fire out? Why did only Lakshmi's pink moon face burn while the rest of her dripped water, untouched by flame? It was a mystery. No. It was a *miracle*.

As soon as this realization occurred to him, Bhupati felt a bubbling excitement, an exhilaration flowing lavalike through his body and spilling out of his sandpaper heels so that he could not stand still. What to do? Pacing and turning and shifting from foot to foot. *What to do?*

Capture it.

Bhupati spun around in his slippered feet and realized then that all the lights in the house had gone out. *The lights are off but somebody is home.* He chuckled to himself at his own joke, squinting as he reached for his jacket tossed over the back of his chair, tucked in across from Maneesha's chair, at the kitchen table. He pulled his phone from a side pocket and held it up to the glass. With his eyes, he could see the fire clearly, but through the phone camera's lens, through the dirt-streaked, rain-spattered door, through the gusting and the pouring and the distance and the dark, there was nothing.

"Bloody useless motherfucking..." Bhupati muttered, jabbing at buttons on the phone, opening and closing his thumb and forefinger on the screen in a futile attempt to zoom in. After several minutes of this, the battery icon began to flash red, the phone went dead, and the fire went out.

BHUPATI TOOK THE streetcar to Little India and bought another Lakshmi. At the Walmart in Gerrard Square, he found an inflatable pool for children, a bicycle pump to inflate it, and in the toy section, a box of wooden fruit. He brought all these things home, and when the back-yard dried out, he set up a new shrine. Maneesha watched from the kitchen, unimpressed. Bhupati thought he saw her mouth moving, but through the door her face was a blur. He put his hand to his ear and shook his head.

"Since when do you pray?" she demanded, sliding the door open and standing with hands on rounded hips. "What's the point of all this?" Pregnancy made her irritable.

It was true, Bhupati had no real intention of praying to the goddess, but he believed somehow that giving her a home, caring for her, feeding her — these acts would be devotion enough to get them to the Hills.

Bhupati waved Maneesha back inside and returned to his work. It seemed wrong to dump the first Lakshmi in the trash, so Bhupati decided to keep her, charred face and all. He placed Lakshmi #1 in the pool facing the neighbours' house, and in front of her, he placed Lakshmi #2, facing straight ahead and smiling, the gold coins glued to the palm of her second hand glinting in the sunlight. He put the fruit—and vegetables, he discovered, upon opening the box—on a metal thali and left them floating for the goddess(es) to enjoy. Sometimes, during the summer, he would bring flowers from Queen Supermarket, rip them from their stems, and add them to the pool, stirring with his feet a goddess soup in an inflatable bowl.

THE SECOND TIME lightning struck Bhupati's shrine to Goddess Lakshmi, it set her hands on fire. All eight of them. The backyard had been blanketed in snow since January and by April, Bhupati had all but forgotten about the Lakshmis, buried up to their crowns, sleeping in the ice. Or maybe they were awake. Waiting.

The storm woke Bhupati and no one else. He shuffled to the bedroom window and peered down into the backyard, all shadows and muck mixed with melting snow in the pre-dawn dark. He wasn't sure when the rain had started, but now it came down fast and heavy, punctuated by a howling wind that rattled the rusty shutters and thunder that shook the bones of the house. The lightning struck soundlessly, a single bolt zigzagging through the rain, leaving eight fires glowing in its wake. Bhupati stared, disbelieving, the breath sucked from his body. How could it be happening? Why to him? Why again? Sweat dampened his palms, pressed to the glass and paralyzed. What to do? *What to do!*

Call for help.

"Manu!" he hissed, turning his head to where she slept soundly, the baby curled into the curve of her breast. They seemed to breathe together, two halves of a whole, taking up two-thirds of his bed, replacing his chair at the kitchen table, a multi-limbed beast, always hungry, eyes on the Hills.

Bhupati thought not to wake the child with a shout, but rather to give the woman a shake. He looked back down at the Lakshmis, whose hands continued to burn, undeterred by the rain, dripping lotus petals that fell away in melted, fuchsia clumps. He backed away from the window and promptly stepped on the hard plastic head of a singing turtle. He half kicked the thing and half slipped, his knee smashing into the bed's footboard, the cracks in the ceiling suddenly illuminated in pale blue light shooting from the turtle's shell.

"Ow. Shit shit shitty shit. What the fucking hell?" Bhupati was yelling, the baby was crying, and the turtle was warbling. *The more we get together, the happier we'll be.*

Maneesha sat up, pulling the small body at her side into her chest before she was even fully awake. Some actions are all instinct. She cast an annoyed glance at the clock, then at Bhupati, then swung her legs over the side of the bed and was gone, the stairs creaking with the combined weight of the two-headed creature's descent.

"Look outside," Bhupati called after her. "Look at Lakshmi-Ma!"

But by then, the only evidence of lightning was an agitated dog and eight blackened stumps.

BHUPATI WENT BACK to Little India and returned with eight Lakshmis—some bigger, some smaller, some sitting, some standing—all draped in red, thirty-two arms outstretched, promising prosperity in exchange for a little bit of faith. He left Lakshmi #1 and Lakshmi #2 in the pool, one blind, both indifferent to the dead mouse floating by, the corncob covered in ash.

Maneesha watched from the kitchen, tight-lipped. She could have married anyone and gone anywhere— America, New Zealand, Peru—but Bhupati had painted Canada with such a magical palette. In his emails, he had sent pictures of forest trails in colours she had never seen on trees, children laughing in fluffy, sparkling snow, giant houses with swimming pools just like hotels. That was the life she had purchased with her plane ticket and her virginity. That was what she was owed.

Bhupati pretended not to notice her glaring. Like the original Lakshmis, he too could be blind. He too could be indifferent. He placed the goddesses all over the yard, in shallow holes surrounded by dirt and stones, so that when the Haitian grandmother looked down from the room she would later die in, it appeared that her pinched-faced Indian neighbour had planted so many strange flowers.

Idiot, the old woman thought. *Nothing can take root in the mud.*

THE THIRD TIME lightning struck Bhupati's shrine(s) to Goddess Lakshmi, it set them all on fire. He had tended to them throughout the summer, rotating an aluminum lawn chair between them to eat his lunch out of Styrofoam containers while the baby went to daycare and Maneesha went to work. Even when it started to get colder and the house was inexplicably empty for days at a time, he had continued to visit them in turn, lighting Maneesha's aromatherapy candles when the sun went down, so each goddess could bask in her own radius of Apple Pie, Linen & Lavender, Ocean Breeze. In the winter, he had dutifully put on his second-hand boots and oversized coat and shovelled a path from one Lakshmi to the next, brushing any freshly fallen snow from where it collected on their shoulders, in their laps. They asked for nothing more.

It wasn't raining when the lightning struck, which might have been why it caught him by surprise. He had been watching for warnings, waiting all year for storms. Bhupati was standing where the kitchen table used to be, reading Maneesha's letter. Maneesha's friends who were married to cardiologists and radiologists and all the other -ists that Bhupati couldn't remember told her again and again that Parkdale was a bad neighbourhood. The listings she printed at the library were for condos in places called Richmond-Hill and Thorn-Hill, sometimes King-City.

"So they are living in King-City and we are living in King-Street. Who can tell the difference, am I right?" Bhupati always chuckled at his own quips, but they left Maneesha's fists and jaw clenching, burning with unspent rage. Stupidity made her furious.

The April sky that morning was the colour of a dirty spoon, distant thunder rolling along its edges. If Bhupati had looked up from the letter, he would have seen the fast-moving flashes between the clouds, may have had just enough time to bring the Lakshmis inside and save them from immolation. As it was, his head snapped up only when the lightning was right on top of them and it was too late to do anything but gape, cartoonish, as it split into ten white tongues, kissing each Lakshmi with fire. They went up in flames as if doused with kerosene, neither awake nor asleep, burning on instinct.

Bhupati wandered outside in his bare feet and surveyed his garden of dying goddesses. He had looked up the odds of being struck by lightning twice and found they were one in nine million. Once was a curiosity, twice an unlikely coincidence, three times, a curse. What to do?

Cremate them. Mark their graves.

He sat in the lawn chair and let them burn to the ground. Maneesha had taken all the Tupperware, but he dug through the trash and found ten Styrofoam urns from which he shook out the cockroaches and rinsed the grease. When all that was left of his would-be shrines was misshapen remnants mixed with smouldering ash, he carefully scooped the piles into their spongy coffins and buried them in a neat row along the fence, marking each mound with a rock. Bhupati knew he ought to release them somewhere nice (Under a tree? Into the lake?), but in this country, people trapped their dead in boxes under the ground and this country was where he had taken root. Now the Lakshmis were burned and buried. The best of both worlds, in the end.

BHUPATI TOOK THE subway to the end of the line, then boarded a bus that crossed into the Hills. He had imagined a different landscape entirely — flowering meadows, castles, kites aloft in cloudless skies — but the Hill where he got off the bus and walked to the return address on Maneesha's letter turned out to be nothing more than an unremarkable suburb, just a little ways north of the city.

He stopped in front of a brick townhouse and stared into an upstairs window where movement caught his eye. A woman in a red sari bounced a small child on her hip, swaying, maybe singing. She turned so that the child's head was obscured and all Bhupati could see was their four arms; two long, two short, all moving as one. A man entered, bent down out of Bhupati's view, and then stroked the woman's hair against a backdrop of blue light. *The more we get together, the happier we'll be.*

MANEESHA GLANCED OUT the window at a blurry figure on the sidewalk. Whether blind or indifferent, she pulled the curtains shut. She never prayed for lightning again.

The Vetala's Song

We followed the river down from the mountains to the city called Benares. Such a place I have never seen. All day and all night, they burn the dead. The men were restless and had coin to spend. Those that returned told a ghostly tale indeed, of a ghoulish creature who exists between life and death, who haunts the charnel grounds feasting on corpses and possessing discarded bodies to roam the city under cover of night. They call it Vetala. Some say it has a soul still, but I know not of any God who would claim such a wretched beast. Yet, this is a land of many gods and what price they might extract to answer a monster's prayers, we will never know.

—Burton's Bestiary, 1882

The river is vast and full of ashes. The rickshaw-wallah warns the foreigner not to drink the water. The woman adjusts her sunglasses, even though the sun has not yet risen, and the sky is still draped in purple, layered with the delicate lace of a pre-dawn fog. She peppers the driver with questions—first in English (with poor results), then in halting Hindi—about the river, the temples that line it, and the pyres that billow smoke across its surface. He is short on answers and only points her in the direction of the ghats. She pays him the agreed-upon sum and climbs down from the bicycle-drawn cart. He will take her no further than this.

I watch, veiled, cursing this half-blind corpse whose body I have borrowed. I see then what I have come here for. Under one arm, the foreigner cradles a silver urn. My kind consumes flesh, not ash, but for the woman in the urn, I will make an exception.

The foreigner begins to make her way down the steps and I follow. No one looks twice at a beggar woman with an acid-scarred face. At least here, by the water's edge, the smell of rot that seeps through the cotton sari in which this body was killed is masked by all the other smells mingling together around me—dead fish and fire, sewage and smoke.

The woman has come dressed in a black salwar kameez. Black is the colour of mourning in the country she calls home. In this country, we wear white to part with our dead, and soon, the ghats will be crowded with men in white kurtas, women weeping, children scolded into solemnity, all there to feed the river the remains of those they loved.

But what of those who die unloved? What of those

whose families cast them out, who will pay no priest to chant over their pyres and see their souls safely off? They are left to the charnel grounds. Not many cities allow such places anymore—abandoned groves of withered fruit trees, where dead bodies are left to decompose, unburied, unburnt. It is unsanitary, they say now. A risk to public health. But in this city, where I was once young and knew what it was to love defiantly, two charnel grounds still exist: one to the east marked by a bodhi tree, and one to the west marked by a naga tree. Today, you would have to be willing to make some dubious inquiries to find these unholy sites. Or, like me, you would have to live there, but I wouldn't wish such an eternity on anyone, no matter what their crime. Mine was merely to love the woman in the urn.

IN THE SUMMER of 1981, Sharmila and I became obsessed with the actress Hema Malini. We bought balcony-level tickets to see her new film and were so enthralled by it, by her, that we immediately bought tickets to see it again. We didn't whoop and holler like the men on the ground level did when she appeared onscreen, sultry in a black sequined gown and feather boa. We didn't have to. It was enough for us to be together in the dark, our damp fingers intertwined, drinking in her staggering beauty.

My family lived in a flat around the corner from the theatre, six of us crammed into two rooms with peeling plaster and spotty electricity. That's how there was money to send me to college. There wouldn't be much left over for a decent dowry, but an educated girl was a good investment for any family these days, or so my parents reasoned. Sharmila's people were in Delhi, so she stayed in the dorm. We took turns standing in front of the fan bolted to the built-in desk, one of us holding a hairbrush for a microphone and playing the part of Hema Malini, the other mouthing the words to her song, playing a smitten Amitabh Bachchan in the audience.

Mere naseeb mein tu hai ke nahi? Sharmila twirling, hair flying around her, singing Hema's lyrics to me like she expected an answer to the question. *Are you there in my destiny or not?* I picked up the refrain, dancing with her on our imaginary stage. *Tere naseeb mein main hoon ke nahi? Am I there in your destiny or not?* I put my hands on her waist and she put her head on my shoulder. It was easy to fall in love with each other like that.

During the monsoons, my mother worried I would ruin my uniform running home in the rain, so I started sharing Sharmila's narrow bed. Even with the fan whirring all night, the heat in her tiny room left our nightclothes soaked through, and eventually, we stopped wearing them altogether. We sang each other to sleep, except when we didn't. At first, we said things like *I'm sorry, should I stop?* and *Is this all right?* until we didn't have to say anything at all. I traced my name down her spine, and tasted her on my fingertips, and every day, prayed fervently for storms.

THE FIGS WERE the beginning of the end of everything, but I couldn't have known that then. Love had made of me something invincible, and I was not interested in considering its consequences. We walked through Thatheri Bazaar, hand in hand, and if anyone noticed, they might have thought we were sisters. Sharmila bought a half dozen figs, so ripe the sap oozed out into the bottom of their paper bag.

"My family says I must come home," she told me, splitting a fig down the middle with a painted fingernail.

"You can't go," I said. "What will I do without you?"

"It's only for a few months. I'll come back." She bit into the fig's pink flesh and smiled, swaying her hips to music only we could hear. *Mere naseeb mein tu hai ke nahi?*

Whether it was desperation or desire or both that possessed me in that moment I cannot say, but in the middle of that crowded bazaar, I turned around and kissed her. I sucked the fruit right off her tongue and it was the sweetest mouthful I had ever known. The fear and the shame that filled Sharmila's face when I let her go were slow to register. I was still basking in the sheer delight that had come first.

Gossip spreads faster than fire and soon everyone knew about us. Sharmila was five hundred miles away in Delhi, so I cannot know what penance she was made to pay. I only know what happened to me. The neighbours said I was unclean, my disease a risk to public morality. The landlord threatened to put us out on the street if I stayed. The police came banging on our door. I was charged with an act of indecency. Those who meant to console called me confused and those who meant to punish called me criminal, and when my father wouldn't pay the fine, they put me in a jail cell for three months. My mother said, *Please keep her there, we cannot take her back.* But they threw me out anyway, when my sentence was up.

Sharmila never came back to the city, never returned my calls or letters. Sometime later, I heard she got married and moved to Canada with her husband. She always had been the better performer between us. What could I do? I roamed the ghats and alleys, begging, praying, always finding solace in the rain. The men who murdered me, to make me an example, threw my body in the western charnel grounds and the snakes that unfurled from the flowers of the naga tree and held sway there asked me if I should like to stay or go.

I'll come back, Sharmila said, before she smiled, before

the fig juice made her lips sweet. *Tere naseeb mein main hoon ke nahi?* "She'll come back," I told the snakes. "I have to wait for her."

"Oh, yes," they hissed. "We know all about the waiting. There are so many of you here waiting to be claimed. Stay then, and join the guardians of these grounds, but know that you will be confined to the shadows. The daylight will reveal your true nature and you will be hunted."

"This is nothing so new," I said. "I was hunted in the daylight for my true nature in life. Why not in death too?"

"Unless..." the snakes said, coiling around my mutilated corpse, "unless your love finds you and plucks you out of this place." They chortled with fangs bared. "Then, by all means, go to the eastern charnel grounds, and be free to taste the sun."

I made the deal and woke transformed. I have wandered the city by night since then, slipping into new bodies at will, snapping the necks of men who realize too late they are not the only predators stalking the riverbank for soft and easy prey. I make madness and mischief and feed on the dead. I mine the dreams of children for moments of joy and they wake howling at the horror of the monster in their heads. I sleep at daybreak in a grave of my own making, with hundreds of others who live here too, trapped between hope and waiting, making our desolate home under the naga tree.

I knew Sharmila had come back because I heard our song, an old song now, seeking me out, calling me to follow a rickshaw to the river. The rider was a foreigner with a familiar face and a silver urn tucked under her arm. I felt sorrow to see Sharmila returned to me as ash, but I was not surprised. She must have known before I did that in order to be together, we would both need to become something new.

THE WOMAN IN black stands on the ghat's bottom steps. She lifts her sunglasses and her red-rimmed eyes speak of grief restrained. She rolls up her pant legs and crouches, self-conscious, as she carefully opens the urn. In this woman's face, I see an older version of Sharmila—what she might have looked like if we had been allowed to grow old together. I crouch behind her and she turns.

She is repulsed by me and with good reason. "I'm sorry, I don't have any money," she says. The sky is turning pink and I am running out of time. I reach for the urn. "Hey!" she cries. "What are you doing?" I let the veil fall away and she sees me. She doesn't know what she sees. She only knows she is afraid. "What are you?" she whispers.

The acid they poured down this body's throat while it lived makes it hard to speak, but I croak out the name for what I am, the only name I have now. *Vetala*. We stare at each other, both with our fingers locked around the urn. Hers are warm and clammy. Mine are very cold. I want to tell this woman about her mother, the Sharmila I knew, who threw her head back when she laughed, sang loudly, and loved Hema Malini and me. But all I can say is *please*.

There is a sound from the bottom of the urn, a faraway voice that echoes in its silver cage. The ashes are singing. The woman listens, disbelieving. She is a reasonable woman who does not believe in gods or ghosts and nothing in the life her mother gave her, in a cold country far away from here, has prepared her for this. "Who are you?" she asks.

I am nameless. I am monstrous. I am dead. I am found.

She lets go of the urn. She lets go and lets the tears come freely at last, released to the river, a part of her now a part of it, a part of all things that she knows now are real. I would grieve with her, had I more time or tears left, but the flesh is beginning to come free of this unwanted bride's dead body and I have somewhere I need to be. She watches me creep away, her mother in my hands, hiding my face from the light. She leaves the city and what she has seen behind, never to speak of it again.

IN THE EASTERN charnel grounds, the unclaimed sleep, while I sit beneath the bodhi tree, the figs it bears scattered all around me. I tear them open, mingle fruit with ash, and eat and eat and eat. I am disintegrating. I am not alone. My body is a song and the last thing I know is sweetness on my lips as Sharmila and I watch the sunrise together.

Dreams of Drowning Girls

In her dream, Meena is drowning.

It's always the same dream — she's kicking and floundering, fighting the swirling current, gasping for breath as she breaks the surface. Then she is dragged down again, always back down, down where the water is dark, where serrated teeth gnash at her flesh until she has been consumed and only her bones remain. Even in repeated drowning and death, there is no escape for Meena. She feels each layer of collagen and calcium sanded away by the scales of deep-sea creatures who brush by, brush her off, brush past in their singular fishy pursuits. She is inconsequential to them, barely a tickle on the underbelly of monsters that never sleep. Right before she wakes, or sometimes as she is waking, whatever is left of her disintegrates into salt.

DOUG

The man in the Lacoste polo buys Meena another drink. He smells like cologne and beer and rests his hand on her bare leg. They are not the only ones doing this dance; all around them, the other animals puff out their feathers, their plumage on full display, or laugh with bared teeth.

He leans in and yells in her ear, "You know, you look like that girl Priya from that show, you know with the nerdy guys?"

Meena shakes her head. *What show? Who is Priya?*

"You've never seen it?" He is incredulous. "You have to come back to my place and watch it. It's fucking hilarious."

He paws at her relentlessly in the cab, half undresses her in the elevator, fucks her on the floor of his condo with his shoes still on. "You're so hot," he says, panting as he pounds away at her, as one might pound a flank steak to soften it. Meena fakes an orgasm at the appropriate time, flopping beneath him, shaping her mouth into something suggesting either ecstasy or fear. She wishes she could be tenderized so easily.

Riding the streetcar later that night, Meena googles *Priya* on her phone and discovers that Priya is both the Sanskrit word for "beloved," and is a character on a popular television show, who, aside from also being a woman of South Asian descent, looks nothing like her.

Meena drops her phone into her bag and breathes in the wet air. This is not some backwater hole where she is mocked and gawked at for where her skin is altered by ink, for how she chooses to feed her desire, for her body, for her name. There are so many boxes open to her now — that's why she came here, after all — but despite all the swipe-rights and semicolon-right-brackets, she has not been able to reconfigure herself in a way that fits. Not yet. Even in the rain, the city is teeming, bursting at the seams, as multicoloured bodies spill from the bars onto the street, cabs converging on every corner to carry them home. Meena closes her eyes and wonders if our names imprint our lives with a certain inevitability, if, eventually, we cannot help but become what we are called.

IN HER DREAM, Meena is drowning.

She paddles and treads and opens her mouth to wail at the sky, but water rushes in and fills her lungs, and she sinks down, all the way down again. She snaps with her toothless gums at the creatures who try to eat her, tries in vain to preserve the meat on her bones. They nibble away (with typical fishy indifference) at the fleshy pads of her fingers, slurp out her eyes with barbed tongues, and when there is not enough left of her to make a decent meal, they move on, seeking out fresher fare. She withers and rots, the fragments that used to form a woman eventually washing up on a picturesque shore, to be shovelled into globes and jars and bottles, a permanent piece of kitsch on a teenage girl's bedside table.

In her disjointed voice, she whispers, "Let me out, I don't belong here."

But the girl never puts the pieces together, and from where she lies sleeping, everything sounds the same.

VARUNA

Meena meets the woman with too-big glasses at the corner of Spadina and College. They are often waiting for the same streetcar and she has attempted flirtation enough times to make her interest clear. One day, Meena decides to take the bait. She becomes this woman's girlfriend. She cooks her dinner and eats dinners cooked by her, celebrates Diwali with her family, watches Bollywood movies with her, and afterwards, lies stripped and spread open in her bed. The woman likes to keep things clean and she takes her time taking Meena apart, picking out the sweetest bits, spitting out the bones.

"You're so different from other brown girls," she says.

"I sometimes feel like I don't belong here," Meena says. "Do you ever feel like that?"

Her girlfriend snorts and replies, "Nobody belongs here. Nobody belongs anywhere."

She means it as a joke, or perhaps as a comfort, but it only confirms Meena's suspicion that it's time to jump ship.

IN HER DREAM, Meena is drowning.

The boat from which she has jumped is sailing away and the sea is pulling her down, down again to where nothing is in colour because there is no light. Her body thrashes and flails even as her mind goes blank and quiet. It accepted the inevitable long before her panicked limbs must do the same. Then, all at once, she is swept up, along with hundreds of others like her, naked and netted, screaming as they are lifted into the sky. All around her, they wriggle and gasp, their eyes bulging, their slick bodies glistening in death. The air kills them even as it keeps her alive. She claws through layers of clammy skin, tears out handfuls of hair, carelessly, remorselessly, until she reaches the top of the pile.

"Let me out!" she calls down to the fishermen. "I don't belong here!"

But the men never hear her voice, and from where they are standing, everything looks the same.

ADRIAN

Meena wakes, not disintegrating this time, but simmering. Buttered and battered, she is all tender flesh falling apart, each morsel melting softly on the tip of her eater's tongue. She reaches with her hands and finds a head between her legs; the wet pours from within her, filling the man's mouth, dripping from his bearded chin. His fingers are slippery from handling her and his teeth flash white when he smiles, a brief warning before she is impaled.

"You're mine," he says.

She remembers she read somewhere that a French expression for orgasm is *la petite mort* and now, with this iridescent man stretched out on top of her, she wants it to be true. She doesn't want to die alone in a net or in a jar, trapped in her bones, screaming without making a sound. *Better to die here than in a dream*, she thinks. *Better to die once than over and over again.*

They take the streetcar together, he on his way to work, she along for the ride. They push to the back where there are still empty seats and sit together, necessarily close but not touching, the memory of earlier intimacies filling in the spaces between them.

"Hey, what does your name mean?" he asks.

"I don't know," Meena lies. "What does your name mean?"

"I guess it's the name of a river or something. But originally, I think it just means 'the sea.'"

Meena looks around and realizes that of the people around them, his is the only white face. In this small herd at the back of the Spadina streetcar, he is the only one not in colour.

"Do you ever feel like you don't belong here?" she asks him.

He looks up from his phone. "Yeah, but I think everyone feels like that." The streetcar lurches to a halt at a busy intersection and the people shift and shuffle around each other as the doors open. He pulls the wire for the next stop and stands up. "Everyone belongs somewhere, Meena," he says.

She watches him descend onto the street, weaving between the umbrellas and the backpacks, until he is swallowed up by a city that is hungry and wet.

She texts him: *I looked it up. Meena means fish. Maybe we belong together ;)*

Later, when she lies down alone in her bed, after he has sent the awkward joke about having too many fish to fry right now, as she comes to understand that she will not see this man again, she harbours the hope that she will dream of him: an expanse of white and blue and blond that she could have called home.

It doesn't matter, she thinks, imagining the golden babies they will never make, tasting salt on her cheek. *He'll be extinct soon.*

MWANI

Meena pushes through the crowd, leading her pack in a line behind her until they claim a circle of dance floor and begin to move to pounding music, all painted in bright colours, each absorbed in her own pursuits. One of them extends a heart-shaped tab on the tip of a finger and Meena licks it off, letting it dissolve beneath her tongue. Everywhere there are hands, boats, nets, glass, and she is drowning again. She doesn't fight it this time, lets the air escape from her collapsing lungs and open mouth in bubbles that go *glub glub glub* as they rise. Meena closes her eyes, ready to die for the last time.

"You don't belong here." The voice of the glitter-lip-gloss goddess reaches down, down all the way to where Meena is caught in the strangling grasp of a pair of eels, and pulls her to the surface where she can breathe again. Off the floor, out of doors, onto a corner where the lights blur in the rain as the streetcars glide past—here is where they stop. "You were dying in there," they say.

There are questions Meena doesn't know how to ask as they link an onyx arm with hers and meander down the sidewalk, then down the stairs, into an underground space where they peel her clothes away. The strong hands tipped in fuchsia, the long hair that gets hung on a hook, the cock, the caress, the music of anatomy that is discordant and harmonious at once—none of these things matter to Meena as she curls with them into a dark ball that opens and rolls and delights to be caught and thrown and then caught again. Caught and held. Meena is unexpectedly content, yet confused. The dream—the death—has been interrupted, an inevitability left unfulfilled. She is in uncharted waters now.

"What's your name?" she asks.

They laugh and there is something new and something ancient in the sound. "Mwani," they reply. "My mother would try to get poetic about it and tell me it means 'One Who Feeds the Ocean' or 'One Who Blankets the Beach,' but, really, it just means seaweed. So sexy, right? She basically called me fish food."

Meena has to laugh too, tries to make the sounds of her name, tries to explain why Meena wrapped in Mwani is so funny and so right. But she is suddenly so tired, the taste in her mouth so sweet, the sound of the rain so far away.

"It's okay," Mwani says, as Meena falls asleep. "You're safe here."

IN HER DREAM, Meena is swimming, as fish are meant to do.

She breathes the water in through her skin as her ancestors have done for a million years. Their fossils guide her through the dark, skirting the teeth and the traps, the piles of bones and the clouds of salt. She swerves from current to current, makes great leaps through cresting waves until she is seen; she shakes the monsters from their caves and vibrates until she is heard. She eats until she is full. Meena swims on and finds belonging in the movement, in the spaces in between. Right before she wakes, or sometimes, as she is waking, she feels the tickle of a seaweed strand brushing by, brushing lips and inner thighs, brushing her dead scales away until whatever is left of her is left alive.

In the Bone Fields

The farm where Devika and Revika were born could not be found on any map. It existed—real as all its broken-down boards and its long-abandoned barn groaning against the howling winds sent forth from Lake Erie to batter the field and rattle the rusty silo. Yet the narrow road on which it sat veered off from the highway like a wayward gravel snake seeking to shed its skin in private. It was an hour's drive at least from the nearest ghosts of civilization, and double that in the winter when drifts of snow made the access road virtually impassable.

The farm hadn't always been in such a sorry state of disrepair. When Devika and Revika's grandfather, one Mohan Chakraborty, had first arrived from Pondicherry, one of hundreds of migrant workers summoned from the subcontinent in the 1960s to work the fields of a barren country turned fruitful for a few blessed months each year, the barn and the house in its shadow had been bright red, shining at the edge of an expanse of green surrounded by a white fence. Along with the corn, the melons, the pumpkins and potatoes Mohan grew from the stingy ground, he nurtured alongside them a budding romance with the farm owner's fair-haired daughter. They were married and the farm passed into the young couple's care. They tried for many years to have a child, with no luck, until one day, while she was weeping in the grass, the field whispered a solution into Devika and Revika's grandmother's ears. She listened, and though she got what she desired, the farmhouse got something too.

Devika and Revika's mother proved to be a flighty creature who left the farm as soon as she could and returned round with twin girls in her belly. There was no record of her death, nor her mother's before her. There were no witnesses, save a cracked mirror and the moon, to a terrified young woman and her father praying to all the gods they knew as two tiny blue babies lay in their arms, cold and silent. Who can say what deal was struck so that in the morning, four dark eyes opened and the house was filled with the cries of newborns, alive and well, wailing their motherless woe at the remnants of the winter storm outside.

In his heart, Mohan knew his wife and his daughter

should both have been returned to ash, the ash released into water, into air. But the fields had called them, had compelled him to bury their bodies, half-rotted by the time the earth was soft enough to open, and he had obeyed. Two gravestones marked their resting place, the only small patch of field he dutifully tended and cleared of brush, while the rest of the land fell to neglect and decay. He shut up the room of the house where the thing nobody saw had happened and set about raising the twins, Devika and Revika, as best he could.

They grew as girls will if left unchecked, curious and bold, two bright flowers reaching for the sun. In appearance, they were exactly alike, but in nature, they could not have been more different. Devika took after her grandmother, capable and quick, born with a love of the farm in her bones. Revika, on the other hand, was wilful and wild, resentful of the ramshackle farm that was not even worthy of its own marker on the map. They took a bus to and from the little country school in the nearest little town that the highway passed, except when it snowed and the single side-winding road to the farm was lost to mountainous drifts left unploughed. Eager though they were to be invited to birthday parties and into town for movies and milkshakes, children have a sense for strangeness, and so the twins had few real friends. The distance others kept drove Devika closer to the land and she grew determined to restore the farm to its former glory. By contrast, Revika grew restless and began to dream of adventures somewhere far away. The farm, for its part, heard the yearning of their young hearts, and after many years dormant, decided to deliver them a gift.

It began during the summer the girls turned twelve. The days were long and they soon became bored with books and bike riding and watching their grandfather mutter at gravestones that were unmoved by his grief. Devika had availed herself of a box of tools she found rusting in the barn and roamed the house, looking for things to fix. Revika followed, sullen, not looking for anything at all, other than her chance to escape. Perhaps that's why the farmhouse chose to make its magic known to her first.

"Devi, did you hear that?"

Devika looked up from her tinkering with the broken banister at the top of the stairs. She cocked her head and listened, then rolled her eyes and went back to her work.

Revika followed the sound, a soft sort of scraping, to the end of the hallway, to the door that had always been locked. The knob turned smoothly beneath her palm and the door swung open, inviting her into the musty space of a bedroom draped in heavy sheets and coated from corner to corner in a thick layer of dust.

Devika appeared behind her, peering over her shoulder. "How'd you get the door open?" she asked.

"I didn't," Revika replied, already making her way into the room.

Devika hesitated. "Are you sure we should be in here?" The room felt removed from the rest of the house, darker than it should have been, even with its shuttered windows, in the middle of the day. A sheet covering a chest of drawers fluttered although there was no breeze, and they both heard again the soft scrape of a drawer opening, then a gentle thud as it closed again.

"That's weird," Devika said, pushing past her sister to pull the sheet away. They watched as the top drawer slid open and remained that way. An invitation.

Devika looked inside the drawer, which was empty, then got on her hands and knees to check if either the floor or the chest itself was slanted. Meanwhile, Revika pulled sheets free of a writing desk, a wooden chair, and an oval mirror attached to the chest of drawers. She traced her name in the dust on the mirror's surface, revealing as she did so the cracks that spiralled out from its center, like a spiderweb woven into glass.

"Do you think this was our mom's room?" Revika asked. They knew almost nothing of their mother, other than where she was buried, out in the field. Revika turned, wide-eyed. "Do you think this is where she died? Do you think this room is haunted?"

Devika stood, hands behind her back, and nodded.

"I think it's definitely haunted..." she whispered, "...by rats!" Gleefully, she thrust forward a recently dead rat discovered beneath the chest of drawers, dangling the rodent's corpse in Revika's face.

Revika shrieked and stumbled backwards, falling onto the bed and raising another cloud of dust. Distracted by Devika's cackling and Revika's complaints, neither of them felt the farm—the barn and the house and the fence and the field—shudder with wanting, barely holding its hunger at bay. But it was a patient thing. It could wait.

Devika tossed the rat into the open drawer and held up in her other hand a small bit of curved wood, flat on the bottom, jagged on top. "It's not haunted, idiot. It's the '90s, not the 1800s or whenever ghosts are from," she said. "The chest is missing a foot, see? That's why the drawer won't stay shut." She dropped the broken piece into the drawer for safekeeping and slammed it closed. "I bet I can fix it—I just need to find some glue. Now let's get out of here before we get caught!"

Devika ran down the stairs, buzzing with the excitement of finding a secret room. Its oddness was due to being unused, and even if the furniture was useless, a secret was a special thing to have. A gift.

Revika stood to follow her sister, but movement in the mirror caught her eye and she turned to look. A flash of dark hair, familiar eyes, a gaping mouth; half woman, half bone. Revika frowned and looked again and saw that it was simply her own reflection, fragmented by cracks. She left the room, closing the door behind her. The glue was forgotten when dinner was served, and it was only the next morning, when their grandfather was tending the graves and the girls could return to the room unnoticed, that they heard the scratching from inside the drawer. Devika pulled it open and a rat scampered out, skittering over the drawer's edge, before tumbling to the ground and escaping out the door.

"I thought that thing was dead," Revika exclaimed.

Devika closed the drawer. "I guess it wasn't," she said, even though she knew that when she had first seen it, it had been dead. It had been and now was not. The dresser's broken leg too was gone, and Devika didn't need to check to know that it was in its rightful place, made whole, or something like it.

"When did you fix the leg?" Revika asked.

Maybe it was because she had been placed in the drawer first on the night she and Revika were born, and died, and were born again (or something like it) that Devika understood the farm for what it was. She looked in the mirror and made with it a pact. "This morning," she replied. "Before you woke up."

So they set about tidying the space, and for a while, delighted in the shared deception of a room that was meant to be locked but had opened, somehow, just for them. They shared their summer secrets there, kept their treasures hidden there, but before she went to bed each night, Devika always made sure to check the top drawer for anything her sister might have left behind. She wanted no cause to tempt the house into transformations that could not be explained.

At summer's end, they went back to school, and the room being just a room in a dilapidated house on a long-dead farm, Revika soon lost interest. The room became Devika's alone and she used it to make the house whole. Into the drawer went the banister's broken spindles. In went bits of faded red board, peeling off from the slowly rotting barn. In went a pair of baby bunnies, mangled by the mower's blades. In went soil and seeds and bug-infested vegetables and bird-eaten fruit, and everything that went in came out the next morning something new, something better. For all these small favours, the house asked nothing in return. It was biding its time, watching the girls ripen.

Years passed and Devika and Revika took the bus to the little high school in the nearest little town. Revika made new friends, age and beauty and distance from the farm all helping her blossom into someone new, someone better. The boy who washed dishes at the town's only restaurant was named Miguel, and when he called Revika on the phone to sing to her in Spanish, Revika felt like she was falling in love. Devika too listened to Miguel's recorded songs and imagined him smiling his dimpled smile at her, and also felt like she was falling in love. But her secret made her doubly suspicious, doubly strange, and Miguel never saw her, never knew how she felt; a weed left to wither in a sunflower's shadow. She was bound to the farm, but she was lonely and wanted what her sister had.

One day, when fog rolled in thick over the field and spring held the farm in its damp grasp, Devika had finished some planting and was returning to the house when she met Revika, skipping down the porch steps. A pickup truck idled in the driveway, filled with Revika's friends, ready to head into town. Devika took a deep breath and mustered the courage to call after her, "Hey, can I come with you?"

Revika looked back at her sister, startled. They spoke little these days and Revika assumed her sister was content playing farmer, hiding in her secret room. She heard her friends snickering in the truck and she hesitated. "Sure," she said. "Go get changed. We'll wait for you."

Devika hurried into the house and stripped off her overalls and boots. She changed into jeans, then a dress, then back into jeans, and as an afterthought, dabbed a drop of Revika's perfume on her wrists, behind her ears. Miguel might like that. From outside, she heard the truck's engine revving. "Wait," she cried, and rushed down the stairs, running out the door just in time to see the truck pulling away. The horn honked and the boys in the back of the truck laughed as she ran after them.

In a moment of desperation, Devika grabbed her old bike from the side of the house and hurtled forward as fast as she could. But rain had made the road slick with mud, and Devika was only halfway to the highway before her wheels slid out from under her, sending her flying into the dirt. Her face hit hard gravel and she felt a tooth jar loose as her mouth filled with iron. She spat the tooth into her hand and picked herself up, bloody and muddy and bruised. "Wait," she whispered again, but the truck was long gone.

When Revika returned later that night, she shrugged her shoulders as teenage girls will do, and said, "Relax, Devi. It was just a joke."

That night, Devika crept into her sister's room, and while she slept, took a pair of scissors to her thick plait of long, lush hair. *It was just a joke*, she thought she might say, smug in the face of Revika's ruined vanity. Yet, holding her sister's hair in her hand, Devika felt none of the satisfaction she imagined the act would bring; rather, she felt vaguely horrified at what she had done. She quickly put both lost tooth and lopped-off braid in the drawer and went to sleep, content in the knowledge that both things could be fixed, and no one need be the wiser.

Come morning, two things were true: One was that Devika's tooth had indeed grown back out of the soft hole in her mouth from which it had been wrenched—but it had been given back to her sideways, protruding from her lower gum at an odd angle. The second was that Revika's hair had grown back too, but not as it was before. Not as it should have been. Her blood-curdling screams brought Devika and their grandfather rushing to her bedroom, where they both stared in horror at the matted ropes of mould-green hair that snaked around Revika's body. She clawed at her scalp and a few maggots fell out, hundreds more still burrowing into the putrid nest sprouting from her head.

"I don't understand," Devika said, but even as she said it, the answer was clear. The hair she had cut had not been tarnished or broken; it had been midnight black and lustrous, the picture of good health. Hunger had begun to gnaw at the house's patience, and with the morsel of hair that it had been fed, laced with jealousy and spite, it knew how to do only one thing.

Devika grabbed her sister's hand and pulled her down the hallway to their secret room. She picked up the scissors and hacked at the hair which seemed to move with a will of its own, the reeking seaweed-like strands winding around Revika's neck. It grew back as fast as Devika cut it off, something stronger every time, something new.

The shutters swung suddenly open and the top drawer slid forward and slammed shut, over and over, punctuating Revika's screams. Their grandfather stood in the doorway of the room he had locked so many years ago and stared at the chest of drawers, at the bed, at the mirror and the face he saw within it. A face that was not his own. "What have you done?" he moaned, and it cannot be said if he asked the question of Devika or of the house itself.

Revika turned wild eyes on her twin, clutching at the hair that strangled her, as her skin crawled with creeping things, falling from her head onto her shoulders, slinking along the back of her neck and into the open holes of her ears. "You did this," she said, and she knew it to be true, just as she knew then why the room had opened to her years ago, and why it would never let her leave again. She saw now what her grandfather saw — her mother's face in the mirror, contorted in a hideous grin. Somewhere behind her, another woman beckoned with fingers made of bone, making new cracks in the glass, the closer to its surface she came. Revika backed away, a Medusa gone mad, but there was nowhere to go, and the hair had wound itself so tightly around her neck that she could not even draw breath enough to scream.

"Revika, stop!" Devika reached out for her as she stood with her back to the open window and the grey sky, but it was too late. They locked eyes in a moment of shared terror, and then, as if shoved by an invisible hand, Revika tumbled backwards and hit the ground with the sickening crack of skull splintering on the stone path below.

The room went quiet. Devika and her grandfather looked down at the broken body lying twisted in a slowly spreading pool of blood. Devika looked sideways at the chest of drawers. "I can fix this," she said.

"No," her grandfather answered. "No more. We will bury her. In the field. Where she belongs. Then we must lock up this room and never open it again." And so it was done. They locked up the room and buried the key with Revika's bones at the edge of the field, now bursting again with corn and melons, with pumpkins and potatoes, and all the goodness the land could provide. Two graves became three and as Devika sat weeping in the grass, the field, sleepy and well-fed at last, whispered how she might be someone different, someone new. Devika listened, and although she got the thing she wanted, she knew that someday, the farm would wake and want something in return.

YEARS LATER, THE Chakraborty Farm had yet another record harvest and the little newspaper in the nearest little town sent a reporter with a camera to cover the story. He photographed the farm owner and her husband in front of their bright red barn and gleaming steel silo, enclosed by a white fence. He interviewed their crew of migrant workers and quoted the owner as saying she was proud to have brought the family farm full circle. Finally, he asked her, "Tell me, Ms. Chakraborty, after your sister's tragic death, wasn't it hard for you to stay here?"

She clasped her husband's hand and said, "Restoring this farm was my sister Devika's dream. Now it is our life's work—Miguel's and mine—to keep her memory alive. We hope this farm will stay in our family for generations to come."

The reporter asked the couple to stand just so and smile, and they did—the man all dimples and charm, the woman a beauty, despite one tooth protruding most unnaturally from her mouth. Upstairs, their daughter, a girl of twelve, rolled her eyes at the spectacle and dreamed of a life far away from the farm. Beyond the house, the field rumbled with hunger and at the end of the hallway, a drawer scraped open, then closed with a gentle thud. The girl lifted her head and listened. Then she followed the sound.

Remembrance

There's a story the local kids tell about a haunted motel just off the highway as you're heading out of town, about the man that was brutally murdered there by his insane wife, about the gunshots coming from empty rooms that still wake the guests at night. Everybody thinks they remember what happened. Everybody tells the story a little different. I remember it too, but I remember it different than everybody else.

I remember how foreign you were, but also how familiar. It was hot, I remember that, and the job was boring as shit, but I didn't mind it because the gas station was air-conditioned at least and it sure as hell beat wearing some dumb-ass uniform and dishing out burgers or doughnuts all day.

The only people that came in were truck drivers or

47

tourists on their way to Niagara Falls. You were definitely not a truck driver, but I didn't peg you for a tourist
either. I remember I thought you were wearing some weird
pyjamas at first—these baggy, bright-purple pants with a
matching top, long and shapeless. Now, when I look back,
I think they might have been iron-creased but who the hell
irons pyjamas anyway?

I watched you walk in and pull a pint of chocolate ice
cream out of the freezer. There were about three thousand
people in that town and not a single one of them looked
like you. I remember you had a long braid that went all
the way down your back and two gold bracelets on each
wrist that clinked together when you put that ice cream
down on the counter in front of me. Big, angry eyes. Like
the princess in *Aladdin*. But instead of a pet tiger trailing
you, you had a little kid. I remember your voice, its accent
when you asked, "Do you have any spoons?" *Foreign*.

When the cops asked me later if I seen you, they
showed me a picture, but there were things missing, things
I remembered. Like the bruises on your neck and the
fatness of your split lip. *Familiar*.

"Yeah, we got some plastic spoons and forks over there
by the microwave," is what I told you. You paid with a
five-dollar bill.

It's funny the things we remember and the things we
forget. Like, I remember that your nails were painted red

and your knuckles were kind of cut up, like you had been pounding on something hard for a long time. I remember you gave the ice cream and the spoon to your kid and sat her down on the curb out front. I remember you left her there and went into one of the rooms of the motel across the street. I forget which one. I forget how long you were gone. I forget a lot of things now, and most days that makes it bearable to breathe.

All three thousand people in that town knew that my mom got hit. Maybe they didn't know how much she got hit, or how hard, but they knew. Maybe they knew and chose not to see. I didn't know anything about you—except what I did, and what I did, I never should have known. *Foreign and familiar.*

I remember the sound of the gunshot. Faint, like someone setting off a firecracker way out in the field. There was no one else staying at the motel, probably no one even at the front desk, so it was only me that heard it. Me and the kid eating ice cream on the curb. Neither of us moved.

I remember you pulled up in a black Porsche. I pumped gas all summer in that shithole town and never saw another one of those the whole time. I watched you through the glass of the gas station door and I knew it was you even though you looked different. You slung that garbage bag over your shoulder and marched with it behind the building, came back empty-handed. I remember you had a nice body, now that I could see it in a tank top and shorts. Long brown legs, choppy black hair just covering your neck. So no one would see. So no one would ask. *Foreign and familiar.*

You put that little girl in the back seat of your car and the two of you drove away, toward the city. When I was closing up, I took all the trash around back and hoisted the bag into the garbage bin. I took a bag and I left a bag and I never told a damn soul. I sat in my dad's car and watched the motel sign flicker for a while, sort of waiting to see if anything would happen, but mostly because I didn't want to go home.

I remember that the cops were over there when I got to work the next day. They put up a bunch of yellow tape and wheeled a body out wrapped in black plastic. Two of them came by with that picture of you and one of them opened up the bin, then they both stood around smoking and staring at the motel. That's how everybody got to calling it the "murder motel." Every town needs a ghost story and you gave them a good one all right. Even today, the kids drive by and shine their phones into the windows, but if they're looking for ghosts, I think they're looking in the wrong place.

I haven't lived in that town for a long time, and I don't think about it a whole lot. There's not much worth remembering. Every so often, I go back to visit my mom, and sometimes I wonder if she ever thought about putting me in the car and driving away. My secret hope is that she has, even just once, imagined holding a gun in her twice-fractured hands.

I usually stop to fill up at the gas station before heading home. I don't have to keep going back there, but I want to remember you. I want you to know I gave you what I could, when I saw, when I knew.

Now I take my own kids out of the city and up to the lake over the long weekends and there's memory lurking in the heat. My eyes sting when we sit around the fire and I remember when I burned a bag of bloody purple clothes, four bracelets, and a hacked-off braid in the backyard while my mom iced a black eye standing at the kitchen sink. I blame my tears on the smoke and watch the holiday fireworks explode over the water, loud as gunshots echoing in the night.

Milk

It was hot, the way the end of May can be sometimes, spring curdled into summer overnight. Anju's thighs stuck together, that fat-girl thigh sweat chafing as she walked home. Her wrist still hurt. She shifted her backpack on her shoulders and got a whiff of the faintly sour smell that clung to the canvas fabric now, no matter how many times Ma hosed it down.

"*Saala kutiya,*" Ma had said, sucking her teeth, after the first time. *Dirty bitches.* She had pushed the nozzle of the hose right into the yawning mouth of Anju's backpack, still dripping with the milk they had poured into it that day. "That *gori* thinks she's better than you? Walking around barely dressed. Thinks she's so clever. Well, we'll see." She had paused, hand on the trigger. "We'll see who's laughing when the wolves sniff her out. Dirty girls can't hide forever."

"What wolves, Ma?" Anju had asked. They rented a small house at the older end of the suburbs, and the only wild animals Anju had ever seen were skinny squirrels with patchy fur and a few garbage-seeking raccoons.

IT DIDN'T HAPPEN every day, once or twice a week if Anju was lucky. This girl January was the leader. Anju thought she was beautiful—pale like a vampire or a medieval queen, with long white legs and long yellow hair. She seemed sophisticated somehow, aware of the world, and above it at once. Instead of a backpack, she carried a black leather purse with a snow-white rabbit's foot dangling from the strap. Even when January's friends blocked the bathroom door and she pinned Anju to the wall to pull her backpack off her body, Anju still half expected her to break out in song like an animated princess, to explain with a smile that all of these trials of milk and meanness had been but a test. And so Anju said nothing, even as January emptied an entire carton of white milk into her bag and zipped it up, handing it back with a satisfied smirk. Maybe it was because Anju was fat or because she was brown, or maybe January did it just because she could. Whatever the reason, Anju felt certain that eventually, if she was patient and kind, she could pass the test. Then she too could become something willowy and white, a January girl at last.

Anju knew it would happen again today, knew from the moment January petted her frizzy ponytail in homeroom, like pitifully stroking a cat's matted fur. Halfway through class, a folded note flew sideways and landed on Anju's desk. She swiped it into her lap and opened it. In her lurching scrawl, in red pen, January had written: ANJU LOVES COCK. ANJU DRINKS CUM LIKE ITS MILK.

Anju wrote in the missing apostrophe in *it's*, then refolded the note and put it in her backpack. Words like that, like *cock* and *cum*, made her burn up, but the fire was contained beneath her skin. There was no modest bloom of roses on Anju's dark and spotty cheeks to give her humiliation away. She could have thrown the note out, but she didn't. She carried it around with her until January found her and shoved her into the bathroom. Anju didn't carry much else anymore. She knew it would all get doused anyway.

Walking home, she knew Ma would be angry. "How many times is this going to happen, Anju?" she would demand. "One of these days, I'm telling you, I'm going to find that *gori* and take her into the woods to teach her a good lesson." But Anju knew these were empty threats. Nobody went into the woods.

Today, January had pinned her to the wall harder than usual. Her nails had dug like claws into Anju's wrist as she held up the note before pouring the milk in. "Why do you keep this shit?" she had hissed, so close that Anju could smell her foundation, see the mottled skin beneath the caked-on liquid coating. January crumpled the paper in Anju's face and Anju thought, for a few terrible, thrilling seconds, that January might make her eat it, watch her choke on this wad of bleached pulp and red ink. Instead, January threw the note on the floor and when the milking was done, she and her friends left, while Anju poured what she could out into the sink. Anju was a shaking a little, elated. Closer than ever, she felt, to some shared secret emerging between them.

THE ROAD TO the house Ma was renting snaked around a narrow creek, a dirty offshoot of the nearby Humber River. The St. Benedict kids came to the creek to drink or smoke weed or make out, but they mostly cleared out at night, when everyone knew pervs and junkies took it over. There was a rickety bridge crossing the water, acting as a barrier to the woods beyond. Anju had never crossed the bridge, but her friend Libby had, once, on a dare. She had gone in and come back out in a matter of minutes, running across the bridge to report to the waiting circle of kilted and cardiganed girls that she had seen *a man*. An old man with dark hair and dark skin. And he had been *pissing*. Libby delivered all this with gleeful, horrified authority, chipmunk cheeks flushed, eyes bulging behind her bent glasses. And they had all looked sideways at Anju because she also had dark skin and dark hair and there was nothing in her, no hint of beauty, wit, or grace, to suggest she and he might not be connected in some sinister way. That had been in the fall, before January, and Anju and Libby didn't hang out together so much anymore.

Anju wanted to go home. She wanted to throw her damp, foul-smelling backpack off the back porch for Ma to deal with when her shift at the Mandarin was over. She wanted to peel off her kilt and lie on the couch with the fan on high, and eat mint chocolate ice cream straight out of the tub. She only stopped because she saw January's purse in the creek. It had to be hers—nobody else had a purse like that. Anju stood on the bridge and watched it bob in the muddy water, its strap caught on a rock, its rabbit's-foot charm half-submerged like a soggy, headless mouse.

She heard a howl. She still wanted to go home, wanted to go so badly, to get out of the heat, but she went into the woods instead. She didn't have to go far. She saw January just off the path, on all fours between the trees. A man with long, dark hair stood behind her, cock in hand, his cum spurting onto her naked back, like a torrent of milk splashing against her skin. January lifted her chin and howled at the blue sky, but the man turned his head. He saw Anju there and he snarled, not really a man, Anju realized. Not really a man at all.

The burning inside Anju took solid shape and rose in her throat and she turned to retch violently into the grass. She huddled there on the ground in the woods, sweat and snot dripping down her face. The smell in the trees, in the dirt, choking her with every hitching breath, was not a smell that belonged in any safe place. She heard Ma's words in her head: *We'll see who's laughing when the wolves sniff her out.* Anju crawled blindly along the path, scraping up her knees, until she could see the bridge again. She got up without looking back and ran all the way home.

The house was empty; Ma's shift wasn't over until midnight. Anju thought of taking the bus to the Mandarin. She thought of texting Libby. She thought of calling the police. But she did none of these things. Instead, she turned the fan on and got the ice cream out and sank into the couch, the thing she had seen rolling around in her belly, like a smooth, round stone.

The moon came out early, a translucent orb winking in the twilight. Anju was eating her reheated fried rice on the front porch when she saw January come around the corner. It was strange to see her in jeans and a T-shirt. Stranger still to see her alone. January was never alone; a pack hunter by nature, a predator by choice.

"You live in this shithole?" She was standing on the

curb, looking at Anju's house, looking at Anju. Although Anju didn't answer, January nodded as if she had. "Look," she said, glancing up and down the street, "you better not tell anybody anything."

Anju still said nothing and January's mouth took on an ugly twist. "What are you, some kind of pervert? You like spying on people while they fuck?"

Anju felt that familiar heat, red pen pressed to her skin, words like blood trickling down her thighs. *Kindness*, she reminded herself. *Soft words.* That was the way the down-trodden in books became worthy of a new body, a new name. Her eyes fell on the black leather purse swinging at January's side. "You got your purse back," she said.

"What are you talking about?"

"Your purse was in the creek. That's why I went looking for you. I wasn't spying, I thought you needed help."

January held up the bag and they both looked at it. "This?" she asked. "This purse was in the creek?"

Anju saw then that it wasn't wet or mud-stained; that the rabbit's foot still hung from the strap, sleek and clean as ever. It was exactly as it had always been.

"I saw it," Anju whispered. "I saw him."

"You saw nothing," January said, and Anju felt the humid air turn cold. The suburban world around her flickered under the rising moon, and she caught the smell of something animal nearby, close but unseen. A final test.

"I saw nothing," she said.

"This doesn't change anything between us," January told her, blue eyes flashing yellow, her face an icy ageless thing in the streetlight's sallow glow. She turned and walked away, lean and fluid, at home in the night. Over her shoulder she called, "Stay out of the woods."

Anju shivered despite the heat. She had seen nothing, but she had been seen. Dirty girls can't hide forever. She licked her lips, suddenly so thirsty, and she wondered if the next time January pinned her to the bathroom wall, they would both smell like sour milk.

Cherry Blossom Fever

MARJAN

Every year, for two weeks in mid-May, the city is struck by cherry blossom fever. In April, the city waits on the edge of spring, which should be soft like rabbit ears or tulips. More often, spring in the city is sharp, the mornings still mean and frostbitten, the grey dusks prickling with the threat of overnight snow. Maybe it's because the city has been cheated out of a proper spring that it goes a little mad by May. That collective frenzy for the surreal, storybook perfection of sakuras in full bloom something between catharsis and cliché.

It was in the midst of this feverish state that Marjan met Talia. She saw her for the first time as the sun was rising behind the trees, which was the only time the light was good and the benches empty enough to sit and sketch. Talia was sitting on the bench Marjan usually claimed for her own, in sundress and sandals, crimson-tipped fingers covering the Starbucks logo on her cup. There were other benches; Marjan could not have said why she chose to sit next to her.

No, that's not true.

Marjan sat next to Talia because she couldn't stop herself from doing it. Like a paper clip drawn to a magnet, she had no choice.

If two people could be immediately reduced to their most primal selves, to their animal brains and strongest instincts, then that is what happened between Talia and Marjan on a bench in High Park, on a Tuesday morning in May. How did they go from pleasant conversation to watching shitty daytime TV and drinking cheap champagne in Marjan's third-floor apartment at the bottom of the Junction? It was the easiest thing in the world. Then later, when the streetcar tracks quivered in hazy August heat and even the shade in High Park felt scorched, it was just as easy to strip down to their underwear and suck on ice cubes while sweat ran down their backs and pooled in the hollows of their throats. And it was easiest of all to dissolve the confines of friendship and satisfy the desire that pulsed between them, a thing as palpable and fully formed as the cherry blossoms of May.

"I think you were born a phoenix," Marjan said to Talia, running her fingers through Talia's hair, which by the fall was the colour of ripe strawberries again. Its asymmetrical lines were sharp, intersecting with cheekbone, lip, and jaw.

Talia gave this serious thought before replying, "I think you were born a mermaid."

And so they mythologized each other with their mouths and their hands and their heat, and as the leaves fluttered down to filter the apartment light in shades of red and gold, it was a dream from which Marjan never wanted to wake.

Marjan didn't think it all that strange that Talia never mentioned her family, who lived so far east they were practically in Scarborough, a world away from the Junction, where they had come alive together. She didn't question why, in the course of a year, she had met only a handful of Talia's friends. People who stared at her with tight, silent smiles, their tongues seemingly swollen from how hard they were biting down. Marjan shrugged these things off, assuming a conservatism that came with Talia's skin, assuming Talia's people would eventually come to love her, just as her own mother and brother and all of her friends had immediately, unreservedly embraced Talia. That was Marjan's understanding of love—that it expanded when you needed it to.

Marjan spent the winter planning her proposal, which she meant to make in the park, when the cherry trees were in bloom again. Under that perfect canopy of pale pink and white, with sunlight streaming down through the blossom-laden branches, she would give Talia her great-aunt's opal ring. She would get down on one knee and Talia would start to cry and everyone around them aggressively seeking the perfect selfie would stop to smile and clap, sidetracked from their quest by a declaration of love born from a fever dream.

Marjan called Talia from the park on the anniversary of the day they first met. She could have texted, but she wanted to hear Talia's voice, her laughter at Marjan's suggestion: *Let's make out under the cherry trees.*

Marjan touched Talia's name on her phone and let it ring.

"Hello?"

Marjan froze and pulled the phone away from her ear to stare at it. Had she somehow called the wrong number? No, it was Talia's number and Talia's face, but not Talia's voice at the other end of the line.

"Hello?" the voice repeated. "Who is this?"

"This is Marjan, Talia's girlfriend. Who is *this*?" she asked.

There was a long pause and then the voice said, "This is Sunil. Talia's husband."

TALIA

I know what you're thinking, but in my defence, it wasn't so much that I told them lies. Rather, I told no whole truths. Is a half-truth the same as a lie?

Where are the stories about me, the ones that tell the whole truth? If I were the main character in an Alice Munro story, I would move to the country and live out my days in stoic, silent grief until I died alone. If instead I were the heroine of a Margaret Atwood story, I would wage war against my oppressors, eventually alienate myself from society, and most likely die alone. If I woke up tomorrow in a Hollywood movie, I would be sad and beautiful and get to fuck everybody, only to be murdered by one of my jilted lovers and left to die alone. If I woke up in a Bollywood movie, I would sing a sad and beautiful song, get to fuck nobody, and then die by my own hand, nobly, dramatically, and (obviously) alone.

These were the words passed down to me by those older, wiser, whiter women who colonized the pages of the books we read in school. These were the stories I had seen reflected back at me on high-definition screens. Even when the language was different, the choices were the same. Silence, rage, violence, death. No happy endings for the deceitful, the lustful, the unfaithful ones among us. Where would be the justice in a joyful end for a character like me?

Think what you will, but just so you know, I was not the only one trading in half-truths. Sunil departed from the script we had agreed to follow years before I did. And if he could do it, if he could mould his body to fit more than one shape of love, why the hell couldn't I?

SILAS

Silas watched Talia's phone light up and vibrate, not for the first time that morning. It buzzed insistently against the bedside table, where she had left it in her rush to get out the door. It was her apartment, her bed, her husband, but Silas had come to think of them as his own. She was never home anyway. She existed for Silas only as a shadow lurking at the edges of his happiness, a distant threat without form or feature. And when Sunil pressed a warm mouth to his, all soft need encased in hard lines and hard choices, it was easy to forget she existed at all.

Eventually, Sunil sat up, forcing Silas's head off his chest, and he picked up Talia's phone. Sunil stared at the screen and when it vibrated again in his palm, he put the phone to his ear.

"Hello?" he said. And then, "Hello? Who is this?" Silas watched Sunil's face in the mirrored wall of the closet doors. It had gone blank, only the occasional twitch of his jaw betraying the collapse of the fragile world they had built. Silas sat motionless, uncertain of whether the moment called for compassion or privacy. In hesitating, he managed to offer neither.

Sunil said nothing to the woman coming apart on the other end of the line. Silas caught bits of what she was saying, enough of her strangled, panicked disbelief to understand who she was. When she abruptly hung up, Sunil put the phone down on the bed, and he and Silas both stared at it, slightly horrified, as if it were a dead rat on the tracks at Victoria Park Station.

Maybe she'll leave him, Silas thought.

"Maybe she knows," he said. "Maybe she's always known that you're —"

"That I'm what?"

Silas wanted to hurl the phone off the balcony and the shadow of Talia, with her beauty and her secrets, along with it.

"— seeing someone else," he said.

The contrast of their bodies side by side in the mirror was stark: Silas was a reed, wiry and thin, a shaggy-haired kid carved from a walnut tree; Sunil was a trophy, formed from molten honey, sculpted into the shape of a serious, broad-shouldered man.

"Go home, Silas," Sunil said.

So Silas got dressed and took the elevator from the twenty-seventh floor to the twenty-second floor of the tower in Massey Square where they lived. He had met Sunil in that same elevator, the only one out of four that was usually working, two years ago. A friendly nod between two brown dudes became small talk, became a beer after work, become *Call of Duty* till two in the morning, then crashing on the couch, crashing in the bed, a hand on a thigh, a need, a comfort, a thing resembling love.

Or, at least, it resembled love to Silas.

At home, Silas ate a bowl of cereal on the couch and scrolled listlessly through Grindr, largely ignoring Cookie's whining and baleful stares. When the pug's circling and snuffling took on an air of desperation, Silas was finally persuaded to switch out flips-flops for socks and sneakers and load the dog into the back seat of his mom's old van. "Where should we go today, Cookie?" Silas asked, all false cheer, ignoring the chasm expanding in his chest, the grow-ing fear that this woman on the phone, with her questions and her breaking heart, had disrupted the unspoken order of things in some irrevocable way. Whatever he and Sunil had, whatever Talia had with the woman on the phone, whatever Sunil and Talia had together—all these things existed in a delicate balance. He knew, with the heavy, word-less certainty of someone who has never been allowed to call desire by its name, that to end one was to end them all.

Talia was always gone, her days and her nights endlessly occupied, caught up in the glamour of her Toronto gallery and the chaos of a city that loomed far beyond the borders of Massey Square. Silas didn't know what Sunil and Talia's arrangement was, or if they had an arrangement at all. He never asked Sunil, "Are you cheating on your wife?" or "Are you gay?" or "Are we in love?" That wasn't the way they talked to each other. To ask those questions would have been pointless anyway. Silas already knew that what he called love, Sunil called a sickness.

What happens when the son of non-practising Christians falls in love with the son of non-practising Hindus? Nothing. Neither family can accept the possibility of love shaped like this; it is simply not what brown sons do. And they were, after all, sons first and men second. Sunil had reminded him of this on those few occasions when Silas dared to suggest something beyond sex, a step outside the frame in which Sunil had them both locked.

"Let's get out of this apartment. Let's get food. Let's go down to the Ravine, anything. Anything you want."

Sunil had looked at Silas perplexed, as if he had suddenly slipped into a foreign language. "You know we can't." End of story. End of script. "I'm married, Silas. What if someone saw us? What would my parents say? What would *your* parents say? You really want to fuck up both of our families for . . . this?"

What is this, Silas could have screamed, but he was easily silenced by stubble against his neck, by the pull of hands that pinned him to the floor, the wall, the bed. By a body that drew pleasure from him like water from a well.

Sometimes Silas drove to the Bluffs, or down to the Beaches, but today he took Cookie to Birkdale Ravine. His phone buzzed in his pocket and he pulled it out to read the message from a recent Grindr match. *Sorry lol not trekkin to Scarberia for brown dick.* Silas barked a laugh. What else was there to do? He walked. When he knelt on the wet ground to give Cookie a belly rub, she mashed her wrinkled nose and frantic tongue into the side of his face. Here, at least, was a language he knew how to speak, a kind of love he could understand.

They came to an open space with a few stone benches and a small grove of cherry trees lining the path to the houses beyond. These were young trees, planted only recently in a neat row. They stood in sharp, artificial contrast to the oldness and the wildness of the tangled woods that sheltered the ravine and its trails. The pale blossoms were sparse and sickly looking, forced to bloom in a place they didn't belong. Somewhere in the city whose skyline Silas could see from Sunil's balcony, its silver towers rising from the lake like so many jagged teeth grinning at the sky, people were losing their goddamn minds for these trees. Silas begrudged them this pleasure, this fever they could embrace, while out here in the wilderness, they burned in silence, never fully flowers, never fully ash.

Silas let the dog piss on the cherry trees and messaged his match back. *I'll come to you then. Meet in High Park?*

TALIA

So you see, I'm not the only villain in this story. Oh yes, I knew about Sunil and Silas. Had known about it since it began. What was it—two years ago now? But I couldn't bring myself to confront him about it, about his "friend" from the twenty-second floor. Was there somehow less room for me in his heart because someone else lived there now too? I don't know because I never asked my husband about his heart and he never asked me about mine and that's how we built a marriage in the precariously safe space of things left unknown. Or, in my case, known but unspoken.

The gallery was already open when I arrived and Ada, our intern, was sitting at the front desk, her phone in one hand, a steaming mug in the other. "Hey, Talia," Ada said, looking up with a smile. "I made a pot of coffee. Do you want me to bring you a cup?"

"Hey, good morning," I replied. "Coffee would be great, thanks." Then tentatively, "Any calls for me this morning? I left my phone at home."

Ada shook her head. "Just Dana and Franz checking in."

Dana and Franz, Gallery 88's long-time owners, were at a yoga retreat in Nepal, but they'd be back in time for the new show's opening. It was a bit gimmicky to do a show of cherry blossoms in Toronto in May (we all admitted that), but it would get us some buzz in the media and get the right people in the door. I didn't particularly like the massive canvases, thick with layers of garish oil colours and gleaming with gold leaf, but I knew Franz was right—they would sell. I sat at my desk and turned my computer on.

Sunil wasn't on social media at all and I had a Facebook account I barely used. Marjan, on the other hand, posted everything the moment it happened. I was all over her Instagram, our curated cuteness a magnet for likes. How long would it take for Sunil to pick up my phone, curious about who might be texting me all morning? It was all there if he went looking: pictures, texts, emails, my whole relationship with Marjan contained in the confines of a handheld screen. Then he would know what there was to know, and I couldn't say for sure if the knowing would be a terror or a relief.

Would they talk? I tried to imagine what Marjan and Sunil might say to each other. I tried to imagine a story, where after their confusion and anger and hurt had been given space to take full shape and breathe, there might still be room left inside them both for me. People do it—open their relationships and negotiate rules and write themselves into polyamorous fairy tales where even the villains get to live happily ever after. Other people. Not brown people. Not people like us. I had imagined the conversations before—the ones I might have with Marjan, with Sunil, with Silas. And the one all four of us might have together. There was no version of that conversation that didn't end in disaster, in utter collapse. Not the way I knew how to write it anyway. Maybe one of them knew better.

"Coffee," Ada said, knocking on my office door.

"Thanks," I replied, taking the cup from her.

"Hey, can I ask you something? You and your husband live out in Scarborough, right?"

"Not quite, but close, yeah. Why?"

Ada shrugged. "I dunno, I'm thinking of moving. I'm bored of seeing the same people all the time, you know? Just going to the same places every night. I need, like, a change of scenery or something."

I sipped my coffee and nodded. I sometimes forgot how insular student life could be, how it could reduce your whole life to a three-block radius. "Well, it's a big city."

"I want to be inspired," she said with an earnestness yet unmarked by the city's claws. Her face brightened. "Maybe I'll move to the Junction."

Everyone thinks proximity to High Park will change their lives, that everything will suddenly be cherry blossoms and coffee tables carved from reclaimed wood, but it is a manufactured magic and nothing is ever that easy. "I'll ask my friend Marjan if she has any leads on places," I said. "She lives in the neighbourhood."

I never told Marjan because she so loves being my guide, the one to tell me all her city's secrets, but I actually lived here when Sunil and I first met. It wasn't as cool then as it is now. At the time, ten years ago, the neighbourhood was unremarkable—far enough away from Parkdale to escape its ramshackle shadow, but not quite close enough to nearby Swansea to absorb its respectability. The rent on my basement bachelor on Roncesvalles was $650 a month and my job at the gallery down the street, my first job out of school, just allowed me to cover it and eat. And that was enough. I wasn't looking for love, but when love wandered into Gallery 88 with the swagger of a Bollywood hero and the biceps to match, I couldn't help myself. I swooned.

High Park is our place—Marjan's and mine. It's where we met, where she first sat next to me and sketched me like an anime character posed demurely between the trees; where I first started improvising new lines when the old script no longer sufficed for us. But before Marjan came along, it was Sunil's and my place too. It's where he proposed.

What happens when the daughter of non-practising Muslims falls in love with the son of non-practising Hindus? Nothing. In fact, both families are delighted. We represented opposite ends of an old country, old words and old wars, coming together on a blank page to say something new. That's how Toronto seemed to us then; a blank slate on which to write our story, fertile ground to plant fresh seeds and watch them grow. The move to Massey Square was supposed to be temporary, but it seemed that while I had been scattering my seeds in the city, planning for a fruitful future ahead, Sunil had slowly been taking root.

When Ada left, I stared at my screen, waiting for a message, a sign, a pounding on the gallery door. I looked at the small suitcase in the corner of my office, always packed and ready, in case of disaster. In case of collapse. In case of today. I wanted to say, *I'm sorry, I'm making this up as I go.* But I wasn't sorry. That shouldn't surprise you. We villains rarely are. We have fought so hard, we daughters and sons of brown parents, to be on the page at all. I am afraid that to ask for more is to ask for too much. I am afraid that to not ask is to close the book entirely. Betrayal, for me, was always a necessary cost. But today, listening to the man I love hum in the shower, getting ready to share our bed with someone else, while I looked at pictures of the woman I love, laughing, trusting, sure of the shape of things in a way I am not, I felt the frame around us start to splinter. In the space of that break, the space of a split-second decision that I could never take back, I left my phone, open and vibrating, on the bedside table for Sunil to find. It would be easier if I didn't love them both.

It would be easier if I didn't have to choose between them. *Silence, rage, violence, death.* It would be easier if there were more choices on the page.

I opened my email and started to type. My message began, *You don't know each other. Or maybe you do. How this story ends now is up to you.*

SUNIL

Sunil sat on a bench in High Park, a phone in each pocket. The sun was starting to go down. The cherry blossoms were in full bloom. A boy who looked like a boy he knew appeared beyond the trees, walking along the duck pond's edge. A woman's shadow fell across his folded hands. A woman who was not his wife. A woman who loved his wife. He looked up at her and choices wrapped in accusations and hurt threatened to spill out onto the grass between them, but he could not speak. His tongue felt riddled with splinters, his heart necessarily numb. The boy was leaving. The woman was waiting. Sunil stood up and it felt like rising from the rubble of a world collapsed and blooming all at once.

"Let's go," he said.

TALIA

The sunset over Roncesvalles had streaked the sky pink and the gallery was flooded with the day's last stubborn light, hitting the cherry blossoms mounted on the walls. They so clearly longed to break free from their frames, the branches painted in bold strokes, snaking out sideways and skyward. Anything to escape the box in which they had been trapped. Sakuras are usually depicted in pastel shades, pretty and gentle, there to briefly please and then gone. But not these. These blossoms were magenta and fuchsia, coral and tangerine, oversized and angry against iris-blue and midnight-black skies, flecked with gold, shimmering and alive.

I lay down on the gallery floor. Outside, the sun sank low and the city went dark, while I lay unmoving among sakuras in shadow, rejecting the colours chosen for me, the script, the frame, the story, the end. *Come for me*, I willed my loves. *Fight for me, fight over me, find space for me, and for each other.* Something burned inside me, rebellious and unremorseful. *I don't want to die alone in this grove of painted trees.* Something contagious. *Find me*, I whispered into the air, into imagined ears and the fragrant, neon night. *Find me and together we'll write something new.*

One, Two, Buckle My Shoe

It started with a whisper in the walls.

One, two, buckle my shoe.

A giggle from the old grate, where Louisa and Raj had set candlesticks in place of a real fire; a sweet, singsong coo in every creak of the old floors.

"Don't you hear that?" Louisa asked her husband, pressing her ear to the basement door, where faintly, from the bottom of the stairs, beneath the rattle of the furnace, she caught again the soft refrain.

Three, four, shut the door.

But Raj heard nothing at all and only turned the radio up, twirling his wife from room to room, the blaring music drowning the house out. There was so much space, inside and out — the perfect house for a growing family. Louisa gently rubbed her swollen belly and felt the reassuring

kick of the life she carried there. Pregnancy must be playing tricks on her, she reasoned, as she followed Raj up the
curving stairs, a can of paint for the new nursery in hand.

It was only late at night, when Raj lay snoring beside
her, that Louisa heard again the house's call.

Five, six, pick up sticks.

She rose from her bed and followed the sound downstairs. On the other side of the basement door, she heard
something like the crack and snap of branches breaking, a
little laugh, a busy hum. Louisa turned the doorknob and
heard the door click open. She poked her head into the
dark and called, "Hello? Is anybody there?"

Seven, eight, lay them straight, came the reply, clearly and
in chorus, echoing in the empty underground.

Louisa slammed the door shut, her own heartbeat
pounding in her ears, and inside her, a faster, softer beating in response; her baby roiling, kicking so hard that the
shape of its tiny foot protruded under her skin. *You hear it
too,* she thought. She rushed back to their room to wake
Raj, to tell him what she had heard, but Raj only said *hush,
hush,* and sang her a tuneless song until both sets of heart-
beats slowed, and her intent to flee the house in the middle
of the night seemed a foolish thought born of a childish
fear. She turned over, touching her fingers to her navel, but
the baby had gone still.

In the morning, when the wind howled mournful

across the hills in which the house was nestled, Louisa woke chilled to the bone. She thought to make a cup of tea and went downstairs, stopping short at what she found. Piled in the grate was a neat stack of sticks. Beside it, on either side, were bunches of branches, torn from the trees, broken down into bits and pieces, laid out straight in even rows. Enough kindling to burn for days.

"Raj!" Louisa screamed. "Raj, did you do this?" Louisa whirled around, wide-eyed, clutching her belly, which was hot to the touch. From the upstairs nursery, where Raj had painted the walls, painted over all the small fingerprints faded into the plaster with unseeing eyes, the radio screeched, drowning Louisa's voice in the garbled static drone.

She cast her eyes upward at the swaying chandelier, where the crystals chimed together, like a child's music box unwound. From between the sticks, she saw emerging small hands, small shoes, small black eyes, a charred face smiling, another, another, finishing the rhyme together.

Nine, ten, start again.

The last thing Louisa heard was the strike and hiss of a match, as the blood ran thick down her thighs and the house went up in flames.

Stories in the Language of the Fist

At the Starbucks across from the Four Seasons Centre, Farrah waited for her grande non-fat chai tea latte. Her phone buzzed in her bag, and she pulled it out. A text from Melissa: *u still there? can u grab me a flat white?*

Farrah looked at the lineup. She texted back the thumbs-up emoji.

"Chai for... Arya." Farrah picked up the cup the barista put down in front of her and took it to the back of the line. Ten minutes later, she carried both cups outside and saw Melissa waving, cut off by the rush of people emerging from the underground entrance to Osgoode Station. As her friend approached, Farrah had a flashback of a girl on skates, ponytail flying behind her. Farrah sometimes forgot they had known each other for so long.

"Thanks babe, you're a lifesaver," Melissa said, taking her drink with one hand and extending the other in a half hug. "Great suit," she said, looking Farrah up and down.

The tailored blush-pink pantsuit had cost Farrah a small fortune, but she reasoned that it was a necessary expense. If she was going to be promoted to management, she felt she ought to look the part. She had paired the suit with white heels, white purse, silk blouse, pearl studs, pink lips, bright smile. Striding down the street, Farrah felt powerful, purposeful, each breath drawn with confident ease. "Thanks," she said.

"Are you ready?" Melissa asked, as they entered the revolving door of the Sheraton.

"I think so," Farrah said. "Although I'm not sure what the point is of presenting to the staff. It's not like they understand the analytics anyway. Wouldn't it make more sense for me to present these numbers to the board?"

Melissa shrugged. "It's a new thing they're trying. The execs just want to make sure that management is, you know, relatable."

Relatable to who? Farrah thought, as they crossed the lobby and headed downstairs into the meeting room. Farrah surveyed the faces, some she recognized and some she didn't — Bill and Mark, Carol and her assistant (whose name Farrah had forgotten), Yumi, who answered the phones at the Mississauga office front desk, and twenty or so other staff she didn't know. While Melissa made small talk with Bill and Mark (her husband golfed with them on Sundays), Farrah gave her memory stick to Carol, who gave it to her assistant, who set it up to play Farrah's presentation on the projector screen.

"There's coffee," Carol said, waving her hand in the direction of a table in the corner, where a spouted box of Tim Hortons coffee and a platter of pastries sat mostly untouched.

"I'm okay, thanks," Farrah replied, holding up her Starbucks cup. "Got my chai latte right here."

Carol wrinkled her nose. "Too sweet for me," she said. "But it must be nice to have a little taste of home for you."

Farrah laughed in the noncommittal way that all non-white women learn to master. Inside her chest, the Fist from which she had learned to hide, in heels and pearls and linen and silk, and all the other camouflage handed down to her by parents who knew what it was to be a target, began to tighten. From the other side of the room, Melissa texted her a GIF of a baby dancing with the caption *U got dis grrrl!*

"All right, everyone, can we take a seat, please?" Carol's voice bordered on shrill. Farrah kept smiling. "As some of you might know, Farrah Chad... Oh, Farrah, help me out so I don't butcher your name."

"Chaudhry," Farrah said. "But it's fine, just Farrah is fine."

"Right, well, Farrah is going to share some of the really great market analysis she's been doing that's going to help inform our local strategy and our expansion out west, which, I think, some of you know about?" Carol glanced at Bill, who shook his head slightly. "Anyway, it's so important to us that each of you feels like you're a part of this conversation, because we all have a role to play in this company's success, right? From our VP" — Carol pointed at Mark — "all the way down to..." Her eyes scanned the people seated in plastic chairs. "Well, everyone." She glanced down at her notes and then back up at Farrah. "Okay, take it away, Farrah," she said. "It's all you."

Farrah stood up, tall in her white heels, and faced the room. Be relatable, professional. Breathe. Be assertive, not aggressive. Breathe. Be yourself but be like them but not too much like them but not too much different. Breathe. It's all you.

The Fist went slack. Farrah smiled and began to speak.

1999

It was a standoff on wheels — Jessicas #1 and #2 on their bikes, Melissa on Rollerblades, and Farrah shifting her weight nervously on the skateboard beneath her.

"So, like, where are you from?" Jessica #2 asked.

"Montreal," Farrah replied, even though Mr. Ryan had already mentioned that when he introduced her to the class earlier that day. "I mean, I was born in Vancouver but I'm from Montreal."

Melissa pulled her hair free of its elastic as she made easy figure eights around the other three. "No, like, where are you *actually* from?"

Farrah froze, not fully understanding the question. It was only as they stared at her expectantly, with their blue eyes and freckled noses and tan lines sharply drawn from summers spent roasting on the docks at each other's cottages, that Farrah began to see herself as they saw her. "I guess...my parents moved here from India," she said. "But, like, a long time ago."

The Jessicas smirked at one another. "Told ya," #1 said to #2, before giving Farrah a once-over that served as both insult and inside joke. It was a hostility for which Farrah had no name, not yet. "We gotta go," Jessica #1 said, smacking her gum. "See ya 'round."

Trailing the Jessicas and skating backwards with the elastic around her wrist, Melissa looked at Farrah with something akin to pity. "She told us she knew something smelled like curry," Melissa said with a slight shrug that conveyed apology and apathy in equal measure. She tightened the hoodie around her waist and turned to catch up with the others, so that they made again an Abercrombie-and Gap-clad trio, sailing together along the Midtown sidewalks on a Monday afternoon.

Farrah mulled the exchange over as she made her way around Deer Park, trying to make the connection, trying to get the joke. It was only on her own front porch that she realized what they had meant—that *she* smelled like curry. It was her. She sniffed the sleeve of her sweatshirt, and then inhaled the air in the foyer as she kicked off her shoes. Her clothes smelled like CK One. The closet smelled like leather and wool and the hallway smelled like lilies from the arrangement on the dining room table.

"Lasagna for dinner, Farrah?" Mum called from the kitchen. "Or Daddy can do tuna steaks on the BBQ?"

"Whatever," Farrah yelled as she went up the stairs. She locked herself in the bathroom and shed her clothes, then stood under a too-hot shower, scrubbing at her skin with a soapy, sea-green loofah. That was the day the Fist materialized from Farrah's ribs and fastened itself around a lung, not so that she couldn't breathe, but so that she would always be aware of breathing, of the way things smelled, so that she would always keep air freshener, deodorant, and perfume in her purse, just in case. Just in case it was always her.

"ARE THERE ANY questions?" Farrah paused and looked around the room. Melissa and Bill were chatting quietly, Mark was looking at his phone. Only Front Desk Yumi gave Farrah a small smile and shook her head. The others were a row of blank, bored faces.

"Well, actually, Zainab has reminded me that we forgot to do the land acknowledgement thing that we said we should do at these things—right, Mark?" Carol looked at Mark, who looked up from his phone, caught off guard.

"Right, sure. Go ahead," he said.

Carol stood up and put her glasses on, squinting at the page in front of her. "We acknowledge the land we are meeting on is the traditional territory of many nations, including the Mississaugas of the Credit, the...Anish... Anishnabeg, the Chippewa, the...Haden...okay, well, the Native people." She glanced up and, seeing Bill tapping his wrist, let the sheet flutter to the table, relieved to be rid of it. "I think we get the gist," she said. "Sorry about that." It remained unclear whether her apology was for forgetting the acknowledgement in the first place, for getting through only half of it, or for subjecting them to it at all.

Zainab the Assistant slid a piece of paper toward Carol, and after looking it over, Carol announced, "According to our agenda, we're supposed to take a ten-minute break. So, everybody, please help yourself to refreshments, visit the loo, and then we'll meet back here for some exciting announcements about our upcoming Employee Celebration Day."

Half the group left the room, and half stayed, pouring the weak coffee and chatting with others they knew. Melissa approached Farrah with a grin. "You killed it, babe," she said. Then, in a lower voice, "Mark and Bill were very impressed."

Farrah flushed with the pleasure of the compliment. "You think so?"

"For sure," Melissa said. "I think *someone* is going to be joining the management team very soon. Oh my god, Farrah, you'll love working at head office — it's literally the best."

Farrah shifted her weight, her pinched feet already starting to ache. "Sounds amazing," she said. "Not that I mind our little Mississauga office. It's like a five-minute drive from the house." She looked down at her phone. A text from David: *How'd it go???*

"We're probably closing the Mississauga office as part of the local strategy restructuring anyway," Melissa said absently, scrolling through her Facebook feed on her phone. Farrah saw her own face fly by, tagged in a picture with Melissa and her kids at Cherry Beach.

"Wait, we are?" Farrah asked. She looked back at the other people in the room. A brown-skinned woman, older than Farrah, darker than Farrah, caught her eye and, for a moment, it looked like she might come over and try to join the conversation. Farrah did not know her and turned her back. She could hardly be expected to make friends with everyone.

"Well, obviously. I mean, they're your numbers, babe. Anyway, I still can't believe you moved out there. Brad and I keep meaning to come and see the new house, but it's such a trek, and with the baby and all, you know how it is. We'll do it though, soon, for sure."

"Yeah, anytime," Farrah said. "David and I would love to have you. Speaking of which, I'm just going to give him a quick shout, let him know how it went." She touched Melissa's arm lightly as she brushed past, noticing the hair elastic around her wrist, as if it had always been there, a permanent fixture for the last two decades.

Farrah took her phone into the lobby and sat at a small table beside a fake forest encased in glass. She FaceTimed David and his head popped up on the phone's screen. "Hey, you," he said. "So, am I married to the new analytics manager, or what?"

Farrah laughed and shook her head. In the bottom right corner of the screen, she noticed the way the light hitting her face made her look beautiful and she turned a little more fully toward the false sunlight streaming into the glass enclosure. "They haven't said anything officially, but Melissa thinks it's a done deal."

"Well, she would know," David said. "Brad goes way back with Bill and Mark and all those guys."

Farrah ran a hand through her hair, her fingers combing easily through the silky, flat-ironed strands. "How's your day going?" she asked.

David launched into a tirade about the inefficiencies of the administration at Mississauga Hospital, and Farrah focused on the way his mouth moved, on how handsome he was even under fluorescent hospital lights. At one point, her face in the corner grew pixelated and froze, mouth half-open, eyes half-closed. Farrah panicked. She didn't want David to see, to think her ugly, frozen face was funny. She hung up abruptly, then texted David to say sorry, the Wi-Fi must be spotty, and she would see him at home.

Farrah stood up and smoothed out her crisp pink pants. In the women's bathroom, she reapplied her deodorant, her lipstick, her anti-frizz spray. She breathed in and out, the reflection in the mirror convincing the Fist in her chest to stay loose. She walked back toward the meeting room, ignoring the pain that every step in the right direction cost.

2009

Farrah met David at a garden party for donors to the University of Toronto Faculty of Medicine. Mum said it was important that they all be there, to support Daddy and say thank you to the people who gave him the money to continue his research. What she didn't say, but what Farrah came to understand, was that it was just as important to be seen at these events, to sip champagne under the white tent in the Hart House garden, to smile and introduce herself, to say, *Yes, I'm very much enjoying the* MBA *program here; it's obviously number one in the country for a reason!*

A couple Farrah recognized from all the donor events paused on their way out to make chitchat, the woman's soft, pale hand on her bare shoulder startling her out of the *Mad Men* episode she had been watching on mute.

"Darling, look," she said. "It's Dr. Chaudhry's daughter, isn't it? My goodness, aren't you lovely. Isn't she lovely, Tom? You look just like your mother, but I'm sure people tell you that all the time, don't they?"

"Yes, thank you," Farrah said, smiling.

"Now, don't tell me, I know your father has mentioned your name before..."

"It's Farrah."

"Oh yes, *Faaahrra*. I just love that. I believe its origin is Farsi, isn't that right?"

"Um..." Farrah paused. To say no would be an insult; to say yes would be a lie. "I'm not sure. I think my parents just liked *Charlie's Angels*, so they named me after Farrah Fawcett."

Both the man and the woman had a good laugh at this, appropriately charmed by the admission. "Isn't that wonderful?" the woman cooed.

"*Charlie's Angels*," the man repeated, looking at Farrah as if noticing for the first time a person standing in front of him. "You know, I find the immigrant experience so fascinating. I wonder what kind of research has been done on how consuming mainstream culture affects immigrants in their effort to assimilate."

He looked at Farrah expectantly and her mind went blank. The Fist around her lung that she sometimes forgot was there began to tighten slowly and heat crept in under her skin, nameless and molten, eager to burn.

"Dad, leave the help alone."

They all turned at David's voice, smooth and cool, like spreading salted butter on an open wound. A sting and a salve at once.

"Oh David, don't be silly," the woman said, and gave Farrah's arm a squeeze before they let their son usher them along the garden path toward the gates where the valet would bring their car around.

Farrah went back to Don and Peggy on the screen, as she waited for the Fist to release its grip, but it was slow to let her lungs fill with air again, and the fire in her veins was not so easily snuffed out.

"Hey, sorry about them." She had not noticed David's

return, nor his outstretched hand offering a flute of champagne.

"I'm not the help," Farrah told him, taking the glass between long fingers with manicured tips.

"I know," David said. He leaned in with a conspiratorial smile. "It was a joke." He clinked her glass with his and they drank together, suddenly companions, as if she had been the audience and not the punchline all along. And because he smelled good and looked a little like Ryan Gosling, she smiled back, and when he asked, she obligingly typed her name and number into his iPhone contacts. She found herself, *Farrah*, sandwiched between Emily B. and Finkelman.

For years afterwards, when David would tell the story of how they met, he would call it "love at first sight," recounting how she had glowed under the tent's white lights, how he had known from that first "cheers" that they were meant to be. Farrah liked this story, fiction though it was. She repeated it to herself often. She posted it on her Facebook page. She texted it to her friends, the same story in different words each time, captioning the cute selfies she took of herself and David at weddings, on vacation, at the Santa Claus Parade. Facebook Farrah has never been happier (58 likes). Facebook Farrah got a new job (75 likes). Facebook Farrah got engaged (192 likes). So when her cousin said, "Aren't you afraid he'll leave you for some white bitch eventually?," or when David's aunt said, "I never believed in mixed-race marriage, but I suppose times change," or when the wedding planner at the Ritz-Carlton said, "We can accommodate a wide range of ethnic appetizers, they just have to stay outside the ballroom or the smell gets into everything," Farrah was ready with her defence; concrete evidence to present to the Fist. The pictures, posts, comments, and likes became an ongoing marketing campaign for her own life, an endless bargaining for belonging that allowed her to breathe.

BACK IN THE meeting room, Farrah sat next to Melissa, a seat away from Bill. Melissa was still struggling to lose weight from baby number two and she looked uncomfortable in the chair, her pencil skirt and matching jacket like a Weisswurst casing barely holding the sausage in. She was still pretty, though, Farrah thought, all rosy cheeks and blue eyes and creamy cleavage straining against the buttons of her shirt. Melissa flashed her a picture of baby number two at the park, one pudgy hand gripping the nanny's dark brown fingers at the edge of the frame. *So cute*, Farrah mouthed.

"Do we have everyone? Mark, you ready?" Carol's voice got the room's attention, and Mark stood up. He was broad and balding, with a face that looked moulded out of white bread, but like most men, he still managed to look decent in an expensive suit.

"Right, thanks again, everyone, for being here today," Mark said. "And thanks to Farrah for such a great presentation. Those numbers are really impressive, and I'm sure we all feel better about some of the tough decisions coming down the pipeline knowing that they're based in solid data." Farrah glanced at Melissa, but her eyes were glued to Mark, as if the words coming out of his playdough mouth were the most riveting thing she could imagine. Maybe they were.

Zainab the Assistant projected a new sheet onto the screen and Mark continued: "The results from our employee survey indicated that you want to see more communication from management and more opportunities to celebrate success. So, next month, we'll be holding our first Employee Celebration Day. We'll start with some presentations from our fantastic regional managers, like Melissa, who I'm sure some of you know. Then, as a way to celebrate all of you, we'll be having a free BBQ lunch."

Carol and Melissa started clapping right away, followed by Zainab the Assistant and Farrah, followed by a smattering of applause from the rest of the assembled group.

"Thanks, Mark, that sounds like it's going to be a really fun and informative day," Carol said. "Are there any questions?"

"Will there be more information about the expansion?" someone asked.

"Will you be closing offices?"

"Will there be job opportunities in Vancouver?"

"How can I move my family across the country? I've worked in the Scarborough office for ten years."

"All great questions," Carol said. "I'm sure there will be lots of information coming on the twentieth."

Farrah saw a brown hand go up and she tilted her head to see who it belonged to. It was the woman who had accosted her with eye contact at the break. Her hair fell past her shoulders (not curly or straight or styled in any discernible way), and she wore a floral-print blouse tucked into ill-fitting jeans. Farrah felt a rush of embarrassment for her before she even spoke.

"Sorry, excuse me, but the twentieth of next month falls during Ramadan," the woman said. There was silence in the room. The woman looked at Farrah, who quickly looked away.

"Ramadan... which one is that again?" Carol asked. She was looking from Farrah to the woman and back again.

"We fast during the day and break the fast at sunset." Silence. "There are some of us who observe this in the Scarborough office. So. It's only that we could not have the lunch part of the celebration. It's okay with me, I am only saying to let you know. It's okay."

Zainab the Assistant pulled up a calendar on Carol's laptop and Carol squinted at it with a sigh. "We could look at the next Friday maybe...?"

"I think Ramadan lasts the whole month," Zainab the Assistant said quietly.

"The whole month?" Carol looked at Farrah, incredulous, as if she ought to be able to refute this obvious nonsense on behalf of her people.

Farrah realized that Bill and Mark and Melissa were all looking at her as well. "Oh, I don't really know," she said as the air around her grew thin. "I don't...I'm not...I really wouldn't know." She was wearing a thousand-dollar suit for Christ's sake. She and this woman were not the same.

"Farrida, right?" Bill jumped in. "On our data entry team? Farrah and Farrida—what a funny coincidence. Popular names back home, eh? Good thing you two don't work at the same office or we'd really be in trouble." Farrah and Farrida laughed in unison, a plastic, toneless sound they both knew instinctively was the right one to make. Farrah stole a glance at this woman—Data Entry Farrida—and wondered whether she too had a Fist clamped around a lung that she sometimes had to talk down from strangling her; whether she might be silently bargaining with it right now.

"Thanks for bringing this up, Farrida. We'll definitely have to think about it for next year," Bill continued.

"Realistically, we can't schedule around *all* the holidays, or we'd never do any work. Although, come to think of it, that might not be such a bad idea. Right? Am I right?" Bill nudged Melissa playfully and she swatted his arm, tittering.

"Okay, any other questions?" Carol asked. People said nothing, shook their heads. "Great, let's move on to our brainstorming exercise." Zainab the Assistant projected a new sheet onto the screen. "If everyone can please move to sit with your assigned groups, we're going to work together to come up with ways to streamline our internal processes and find efficiencies in our local teams. Put your thinking caps on!"

Carol taped up chart paper around the room and handed out coloured Sharpies as people shuffled around each other, dragging their chairs into groups. Bill, Mark, and Melissa stood together at the back, chatting and sipping their coffees. Farrah went to join them.

"Terrific work today, Farrah," Mark said.

"Didn't I tell you she's amazing?" Melissa gushed, putting her arm around Farrah's waist. "Farrah and I go way back, like all the way to grade school. I remember the first day we met and just knowing right away that we were going to be friends for life."

Farrah thought back to that first day of school, of Melissa and the Jessicas circling her, of the appearance of the Fist. *She told us she knew something smelled like curry.*

She wondered if Melissa believed the story she was telling or if she knew it to be a fiction. It was possible her parents had handed down a different kind of camouflage to her. *I see you*, Farrah thought, smiling at her friend. "Who would have guessed we'd be working together twenty years later?" she said. *Do you see me?*

"Speaking of work," Bill said, "I think your group might be waiting for you, Farrah."

Farrah turned and saw that she had indeed been placed in an efficiency brainstorming group. She found her name, *Chaudhry, Farrah*, sandwiched between *Alvarez, Ricky*, and *Duong, Yumi*, and for a brief, breathless moment, she was back in the tent, David's phone hot in her hand, the Fist tight and ready to strike. *Bill*, she could have said, *leave the help alone.* At least she'd be in on the joke this time.

Carol joined their circle and handed Mark a manila folder and Farrah's memory stick. "I'm going to head back to the office," Mark said. "I'm looking forward to sharing these numbers at the next board meeting."

"I'd be happy to do my presentation again for the board," Farrah said. "You know, to give the numbers some context, if you think that would be helpful."

Mark shook his head. "I don't think that's necessary. We really just wanted to get you interacting with the staff. It's so important to have someone like you communicating with them. Someone they can relate to."

"I'm going to head out too," Bill said. "Tell Brad he's got to work on that swing before Sunday," he told Melissa.

Melissa laughed. "He's hopeless!" she replied. "Say hi to that gorgeous wife of yours for me, all right?"

Their circle broke with goodbyes all around. Melissa went into the lobby to take a call and Farrah joined Front Desk Yumi and Stockroom Ricky and the rest of her assigned group to brainstorm ways to make their jobs obsolete. Each group presented their ideas and when they were done, Carol collected the sheets of chart paper, rolled them up carefully to return them to head office, where they were never seen again.

Around noon, Carol called a break for lunch and everyone filed out of the meeting room. Melissa stood at the door chatting with people as they left, asking about their kids, joking about the weather. She was a good manager like that. Farrah stood just behind her, a smiling, well-dressed shadow. As Data Entry Farrida walked past them, they both caught the faint scent of incense and fried onion clinging to her clothes. Farrah drew in her breath sharply. Her house had never smelled like that. Breathe. Her parents had known how to belong. Breathe. It had never been her. Breathe. And it never would be.

"It was nice to meet you," Farrah blurted even though they hadn't met at all, not really.

Data Entry Farrida looked at Farrah and nodded,

expressionless. Then she disappeared into the crowd in the hotel lobby, scattering with the others, absorbed by the downtown city streets.

"Where do you want to go for lunch?" Melissa asked, as they paused outside the plastic forest encased in glass.

Farrah looked at the outline of her reflection. She took a deep breath. "Do you actually remember the first time we met?" she asked.

"Of course," Melisa replied. "Mr. Ryan's class, first day of grade seven."

"You were pretty mean to me that day."

"Really? I don't remember that."

"If I'm being honest, I'd say you and your friends were maybe even being a bit...racist."

"What! Oh my god, Farrah, seriously?"

"You said I smelled like curry."

"I said that?"

"Someone said that."

Melissa laughed, discomfort discolouring the edges of the sound. "Well, I don't know, Farrah, maybe you did back then or maybe kids just say dumb things. As if you've never said anything dumb. Come on though, you know Brad and I aren't like that. We don't even see colour."

"What about Bill and Mark? Do you think they see colour?"

Melissa bristled, indignant at what she perceived to be a trick question. "I don't know what you mean. They're really great guys," she said. "Did you look around that room today? Isn't it obvious how important diversity is to them?"

Farrah pictured Stockroom Ricky and Front Desk Yumi and Zainab the Assistant and Data Entry Farrida eating their free hot dogs while mired in a growing pit of minimum-wage muck. And then she pictured herself, Management Potential Farrah, climbing free of the pit, free of the Fist, free to speak and to see and be seen at last. "Yes," she said. "Yes, it is."

"Anyway, grade seven was a long time ago. Things are better now. Aren't they?"

"Yes," she said. "Yes, they are."

After a pause, Melissa said, "But still, I'm sorry if you took any of that stuff personally, Farrah. You know we didn't mean it that way."

It's no big deal, I've just been asking for permission to breathe every day for twenty years. "It's no big deal," Farrah said. "Really, it's fine."

"Okay," Melissa said. She took a breath as the unfamiliar, unpleasant tightening sensation in her chest began to subside. "Hey, what are you and Dave doing for the long weekend? We were thinking of having people up to the cottage. Bill and his wife might come—she's a sweetheart, you'll love her. You guys should totally come!"

Farrah watched the fake stream trickle peacefully through the fake forest behind the glass. Then the light shifted and she turned away, in case it made her reflection ugly, in case it showed her a kid on a skateboard, a girl under a tent, a woman in a designer suit, frozen in time, all of them with mouths half-open, all of them with eyes half-closed. They were all her. They always had been. And they always would be.

Farrah smiled at her friend. "That sounds perfect," she said. "Thank you." They walked out together, laughing, turning heads with their beauty. Inside Farrah's chest, the Fist curled its fingers loosely around her lung, a permanent part of her anatomy now, and waited for its chance to close around her heart.

Night Zoo

W e left the city for the small town at the edge of a lake because the city had become a dangerous place.

"It's like a zoo!" Amma complained to Appa for months before we finally moved. "We came here so Rohit could have a better life, a safer life than what we knew back home — but now, just look!" She would thrust the morning paper under his nose, jabbing a finger at the latest offending headline. "Every day someone gets shot, someone gets robbed, someone gets raped..."

"Please, let's be civilized at the breakfast table." Appa's protests were always gentle, one hand patting Amma's arm reassuringly, the other pushing the newspaper away.

I cleared my throat, wary of the crack and waver that had found its way into my voice since we had abandoned our life in a city of mountains and machine guns, of funeral pyres that never stopped burning. "Do I get a say in this decision?" I asked them, and was soundly ignored. I expected that: once Amma got an idea in her head, she would never let it go. Look at these pictures of the small town, she said. She knew other people who had moved to the small town and they loved it there, she said. Everyone loves it there, and we will too. The small town is safe. There is no crime. There is a lake. We should go. And then eventually, we *must* go.

The small town was not so far from the city, and we drove there in the daytime to look at the houses we could buy and call our own. Big houses. Green grass. Boats on the water and kites in the air. And the people — *my god* — the people were the friendliest, happiest people we had ever seen. They loved the small town and they loved us and they wanted us to stay. We visited again and again, always in the daylight. We were so charmed. The small town was not like either city we had called home before, not like any city, anywhere. And so, we stayed. Amma and Appa bought a house with a pear tree and a crystal chandelier. Our new neighbours waved to us as we carried our boxes in from the truck. Amma waved back, then nudged me on her way into the new house. "They seem nice," she said. "Try to make friends."

I sighed, so put upon. "What's the point? We probably won't stay here long either."

The neighbours stood on their porch, watching us, for a long time that day. But where Amma saw welcome in their eyes, I saw something else; something like a warning we did not yet know we ought to heed. That was years ago, and the small town is still our home, and I know now it will be our home until we die. Because we stayed. Because we had seen violence and the promise of safety dulled our senses against the faint smell of blood that lingered in the air. Because we made our decisions during the day. It was only at night that the small town revealed its secret. And now, it will never let us leave.

Here is what happened on our first night in our new house in the small town: The sun went down and there was no moon, no stars, no light at all. That first night, we thought it must be a power failure. We didn't know better. We hadn't yet changed.

I don't remember how the change came upon me — I only know I woke up in that thick darkness and I was very hot and very hungry. My body was sleek and soft, my ears sharp, my tail supple. I trotted down the hallway and barked, and Amma and Appa barked back. Then we three, our pack, ran out into the night and we saw our neighbours lumbering by, their great bear paws flattening the grass of our new lawn. We came upon a family of ferrets, one of whom, by day, had sold us our house in the small town, and together, Amma, Appa, and I tore her apart and ate her—fur and heart and fear-glazed eyes and all. We sniffed our way to the water and drank, licking the blood from our paws. It was Appa who turned his head to the sky and started howling first, but Amma and I joined him, soon enough.

TODAY, WE WATCH you and your family arrive in the small town, shading your eyes from the sunlight sparkling off the lake. We are walking along the pier with the neighbours, eating ice cream and laughing. We are all uncaged here; the night alone is trap enough.

You stop us and ask, "Excuse me, do you live here?" And then, "Do you like it here?" You have four children, you say. You don't feel like the city is safe for them anymore. You're thinking you should move.

We all smile at you, teeth flashing. "Oh yes, you *must* move," Amma says. "The people are so kind here, so... civilized." *Four children!* Our mouths are already watering. "We love it here. And so will you."

Arvind

"**D**o you ever think about Arvind?"

Madhuri and Ashutosh are in bed when he asks this of her, as he does from time to time, always in the dark, as if he knows it is too fragile a thing to bring up in the light.

Madhuri strokes their daughter's dark curls, damp against her forehead as she sleeps between them. "We have Maya to think about now," she replies.

It's not exactly an answer to the question, but it must be answer enough, because he murmurs *haan, haan, sach hai.* Yes, yes, that's true. Madhu knows he still keeps the grainy black-and-white ultrasound picture from all those years ago folded in his wallet, the crease permanently bisecting the writing on the back where she had scrawled *Arvind?* in blue pen.

Things are different now than they were then. Eight years ago, Ashu was working three jobs and Madhuri was just trying to graduate. Sometimes, between finishing his shift at the twenty-four-hour McDonald's at Queen and Spadina, and starting his shift at Little India Food Mart, he would meet her on campus, bag of Big Macs clutched in one hand, cigarette dangling from the other. They would sit on stone ledges, kiss with their backs to the ivy creeping up the walls. In temple, Madhu would watch his fingers hover over the flame of a *diya* held by the priest and imagine them moving between her legs. When Madhu's dorm mostly emptied out for spring break, she and Ashu roamed the halls hand in hand, heedless of who saw them. She let him into her bed and her body. They played old Bollywood movies, played truth or dare, played with their imagined future together like a Rubik's Cube, spinning the colours recklessly, all passion and no plan.

Getting pregnant was stupid. Trying to hide it for so long, hoping it would simply go away, more stupid still. When Madhu finally told Ashu the truth, on the porch of the house he shared with four other coders from back home, she threw up over the railing, shaking and crying, gripping the rusted iron hard enough to hurt. She imagined him saying *stupid girl*, saying *liar*, saying *slut*. But instead, he put his arm around her and said, *Sab theek ho jayega, Madhu*. Everything will be all right.

Ashutosh called in sick to the Food Mart and came with Madhuri to her ultrasound appointment at Women's

College Hospital. They heard Arvind's heartbeat for the first time together. They walked along the waterfront, passing the black-and-white Polaroid back and forth, still glossy and unmarked. It was only at the next ultrasound that they found out their baby was a boy, only then that she scratched his name across the back of the picture. *Arvind?* Still only a question hanging in the air, not a fact, not yet.

There were other appointments after that—blood tests, and stress tests, and tests for diseases they hadn't known they ought to fear. Ashu insisted on coming to all of them and Mr. Singh, who owned the Food Mart, got angry that he kept missing shifts. Kevin, his manager at the McDonalds', said that he was sorry about Mad-oo-ree being knocked up and all, but they'd have to let him go if he was late again, and his housemates said, "Look, *yaar*, we're on a deadline. If the investor walks, we're all screwed. Just code faster, okay?"

Madhu tried to go to class, to read, to keep up, but the voice in her head became a brick wall that nothing could pass through. *Stupid girl*, it said. *Stupid to let it happen, to keep it, to love it, stupid all around. What will you do now?* She didn't know. She couldn't go home—her parents would sooner have seen her dead than face the shame that Arvind would bring to the family. And even if she and Ashu could get their own place—after rent and bills and food and things for the baby, what would they have left to build a life with? *Stupid girl*, even as Arvind grew from a pomegranate seed to a pear to a pineapple inside her. *Stupid girl*, even as her professors threw sidelong glances in her direction and quietly suggested she make an appointment with an advisor before she was placed on academic probation. *Stupid girl*, even as Ashu lost two jobs out of three and grew thinner each day, his body hollowing out directly in proportion to hers expanding.

The only smart thing Madhuri did was to call the number a well-meaning auntie pressed into her hand in the temple parking lot one night. "She is wanting baby for so long now, so much prayers, but…" The auntie waggled her head and her hand in unison, in a universal gesture that might have meant yes or no or who knows. "They have big house, big money, husband has very big job."

Madhu watched her breath crystallize as the auntie, whose name she couldn't quite remember, patted her arm through her too-thin coat. In the absence of her actual mother, all the aunties dotting the temple halls blended into the same voice, the same shape. "Think, Madhuri. Maybe this is blessing for you both."

For the first time in months, the voice in Madhu's head went quiet. "Thanks, Auntie," she said. She leaned into her warmth as the kids lit their sparklers and raced around the lot, too cold and full of Diwali sweets to stay still.

⌒

"MUMMY, IT'S MORNING now!" Madhuri opens her eyes to find Maya's face an inch away from hers.

"Are you sure? I think it's still night." Madhu closes her eyes and pretends to snore while Maya dissolves into fits of giggles and shakes her, crowing, "Wake up, Mummy! Wake up, wake up!"

Eventually, Madhu lets her daughter drag her out of bed and they pad down the hallway, into the condo's kitchen. She pours cereal and milk into a plastic bowl for Maya, and coffee from the pot into a mug for herself. On the balcony, Ashu has his headset on and the laptop open. He gestures and laughs, cigarette in one hand, coffee cup in the other. Madhu knocks on the glass door and fixes him with a stern look. He returns it with a sheepish grin, immediately crushing the cigarette in the ashtray, then sticks his tongue out at Maya while she does the same to him.

Madhu kisses Ashu goodbye, drops Maya off at daycare, and heads to the lab, but the question asked and unanswered sits like a cinder block on her chest all day. *Do you ever think about Arvind?* She knows if she doesn't put these bricks down, they will start to pile up and she cannot risk the wall forming around her again, trapping her inside with only that voice for company. *Stupid girl*, it whispers still, when it knows she is listening. *Selfish girl. Traded a child for a fat cheque. You didn't build a life, you bought one.*

They did everything legally, all on the up and up. They are not to have contact with the child, but once he turns eighteen, he can access his adoption file and find out who they are. If he wants to know.

"Hey, Sheila, is it all right if I leave early?" Madhuri makes her face look slightly pained. "I feel a bit nauseous."

Her supervisor gives her a concerned frown from behind her desk. "Of course, Ree. Go home," she says. Then her expression brightens and her pencil-thin eyebrows shoot skyward. "Are you pregnant? I bet Maya would love a sister or brother!"

Madhu rides the subway up to York Mills, as she does from time to time, always in the daylight, as if she knows it is a thing too close to a crime to try in the night. She makes this trip whenever the voice makes it hard to hear or the weight makes it hard to breathe. How can a thing that is not hers to hold still be so heavy? She walks along a winding street, lined with shiny cars and littered with magnolias. There are no men sleeping on sewer grates here, no honking or shouting. Even the grass between the driveways gleams.

She pauses across the street from a sprawling white house and takes out her phone. Just a woman walking, talking to someone she knows.

She waits.

At 3:32 p.m., a boy careens around the corner on a bike. He leaves it on the lawn in front of the house, locked to nothing, unfastens his helmet, and tosses it on the ground. He runs a hand through dark curls and she can feel them on her fingertips, sweaty and soft, and everything is sunshine and open space and silence around her. Her eyes are wet, her body weightless. For a few moments, she breathes the same air as her son, who has a different name now, whom she gave away. Her Arvind, a living boy who haunts her heart, whom she thinks about every day.

Chitra
(Or: A Meteor Hit the Mall
and Chitra Danced in the Flames)

Chitra smoked her last cigarette next to the food court Dumpsters and ground the blackened butt into the pavement with a sneakered heel. Sweat darkened the armpits of her uniform and beaded on her forehead, trapped in her hairnet's elastic embrace. A pale sky above churned with the heat, making the parking lot hazy, but the clouds remained closed. Movement at the Dumpster's edge caught Chitra's eye. Two ears and a pointy nose appeared, there only for a moment and then gone, burrowing again into the fetid depths of the fast-food trash. Once upon a time, she had been scared of the little beasts that scurried around the Dumpster, horrified by their patchy fur and twitching hands, their thick worm tails. Now, she knew them by name. Her eyelids drooped.

"Break's over, princess. Back on the cash." Fern, Chitra's supervisor, held the employee entrance door half-open, trying to expose as little of her leathery skin to the heat as possible. Chitra turned her head and squinted, but Fern had already retracted her turkey neck and only her forearm holding the door was still visible. Chitra read the faded script tattooed there, the words nearly lost in Fern's sleeve of hearts and skulls and snaking vines: *A dream is a wish your heart makes.* She followed Fern into the underbelly of the mall.

They walked the fluorescent corridor together, blasted by cold air tinged with stale grease. Fern paused at the next set of doors. She placed both hands on the bar to open them, and for a few seconds, she and Chitra stood there, savouring the cool and the quiet. Sometimes, in those moments, Chitra imagined a wasteland on the other side of the doors: charred pits where the semicircle of food vendors used to be, plastic tables and chairs reduced to piles of cinders, the pestilence of sour teens and slack-jawed seniors obliterated forever. But the mall had been there for fifty years, had survived floods and fires and bore stoic witness to all manner of petty crimes, cruelties, and heartbreaks. It would not be destroyed so easily.

Chitra and Fern crossed the food court and went back to work. Fern retrieved her clipboard from the kitchen wall and checked off Chitra's break, while Chitra took her place behind the cash register, nodding at the next person in line. Her shift had started before the sun was up and by this time of day the customers all started to blend into the same hungry, open-mouthed shape.

"Hey, big sis." Chitra blinked and a familiar face came into focus.

"Hey, Gauri," Chitra mumbled in reply.

"Just a steeped tea for me," Gauri said, tossing her ringlets and wrinkling her hook nose, as she took in the screens behind Chitra's head where the menu was displayed, each item listed with its caloric value. "How can food even *have* so many calories?" she asked aloud, presumably speaking to Chitra, although the question was for all to hear. Gauri eyed Chitra, lumpy and frumpy in her uniform, and clicked her tongue. "You really need to take better care of yourself, Chitra," she said. "You know how Mother and Father worry about you."

Your father, Chitra thought. *My father is dead, so he probably worries less.* She fiddled with the lily pendant she wore around her neck, a cheap but pretty trinket bought for a child, a final gift from a dying man. It was the only thing Chitra had left of her father. That and the cigarettes. They had been a hand-me-down habit from him too. She thought of the glazed doughnut and black coffee that had been her breakfast. "I quit smoking," she offered, shifting her weight. No matter how many orthopedic inserts or massage-gel insoles she tried, she could never find shoes that fit properly. Her feet always hurt.

Gauri rolled her eyes. "We'll see how long that lasts."

"Hey, big sis! Hey, twin sis!" Dhamini's painted face popped up next to Gauri's like a clown head on a spring. The beauty store where she worked required employees to wear a minimum of seven cosmetic products during all shifts, but Dhamini's interpretation of the requirement always landed somewhere between the comic and the bizarre. She batted her false lashes and pouted her pearlescent pink lips. "Who wants to treat Dhamini to an iced cap?" Irritation so fierce it bordered on nausea bubbled up in Chitra, as it did every time her stepsister referred to herself in the third person. *Who wants to give Dhamini a ride to the mall? What has Dhamini done with her phone? Dhamini sure could use help with this spreadsheet.* Chitra placed the tea and the frozen drink down on the counter. "Thanks, Chitters. You're a peach," Dhamini said, and Chitra watched them walk away together. Fern had covered Chitra's breakfast, and she could count the tea as her one free hot beverage per shift, but the iced cap would come out of Chitra's pay.

They were always short-staffed and Chitra always stayed late, partially so Fern could go home to her kids, and partially so Chitra could avoid going home. *Living with your sisters will be fun*, her mother had said. *You're the eldest, Chitra. It's your responsibility to look after them*, their father had said. And she always had—had been there to sing them back to sleep when the rumble of a far-off meteor shower frightened them awake, and later, to do their forgotten homework and forge their absence notes when her stepsisters had cut class together. It should have made them close, but they were never meant to be a trio and Chitra was always the odd one out. She thought of the greasy dishes that would no doubt be piled up in the sink by the time she got home, the baskets of dirty laundry, the dirty microwave, the dirty toilet; and her sisters, shut up in their rooms, on their phones, scrolling and swiping and snarking and shrieking at each other through the walls.

They shared a two-bedroom grey-brick townhouse, crumbling behind an iron gate, a narrow afterthought tacked on at the end of the townhouse row. Because their father had bought the house, it seemed only fair that Gauri and Dhamini should get the two rooms. Chitra got the pullout couch in the basement, next to the furnace, where it was always too hot, and she was never sure if it was night or day. All she wanted was a small space to call her own, with a window to the open sky and just one pair of shoes that actually fit.

CHITRA ARRIVED AT the mall the next morning, as usual, when it was still dark. The stores wouldn't open for another two hours, but the food court was the first thing to open and the last thing to close. Early-morning commuters cut through the mall on their way to and from the subway trains, stopping for coffee and doughnuts and breakfast burritos on their way. Chitra paused outside the employee entrance, reaching instinctively into her bag for her cigarettes before remembering she had none left and that she had promised herself yesterday's smoke would be her last. She scanned the sky for signs of movement, but all was deathly still. Like everyone else, she had stopped paying attention to the meteor warnings that scrolled like ticker-tape across the bottom of their television screens. There hadn't been a meteor shower in over a decade and the warnings were always false alarms.

The sunrise washed the mall in a spray of pink, a thin spatter of blood light across the concrete walls. From underneath the Dumpster, Chitra heard a scraping sound, and when she bent to look, saw the skinny white rat she called Tinkerbell—the one missing half an ear—struggling to pull a chicken bone from its partially crushed bucket. Chitra reached for the bone and Tinkerbell scuttled backwards, nose twitching, eyes glowing red in the shadows. Chitra yanked the bone free and flicked it toward the rat, who snatched it between her four-clawed front paws and disappeared into the dark.

Chitra saw Fern's station wagon pull in at the back of

the lot, and watched her stocky frame advance, bleached hair spiky so that she looked like a peroxide-blond hedgehog in polyester pants. "Didja hear the news?" Fern asked, slightly out of breath, squinting at Chitra as she punched in the code to open the door without even looking at the buttons. "The Shoe Chateau is closing."

Fern's words hit Chitra like a punch to the gut and she gulped in air as if she had momentarily forgotten how to breathe. "Why?" she asked, hurrying after Fern down the long hallway to the food court. "When? How do you know?"

"Couple weeks. Notice went out to all managers." They went through the double doors, where a handful of impatient patrons were waiting for the coffee to brew. Chitra counted the float and opened the cash, trying to make sense of the sorrow that the impending loss of the Shoe Chateau had stirred in her. She rarely shopped for clothes—all she wore was her uniform or pyjamas anyway. She had no interest in housewares or sportswear, fancy chocolates, overpriced purses, or electronics. She steered clear of the beauty store where Dhamini worked and the athleisure store where Gauri worked. The only shops Chitra visited were the bookstore and the Shoe Chateau.

There were other shoe stores in the mall, but the Shoe Chateau was more than just another store—it was an oasis. Crossing its threshold beneath the neon script sign,

Chitra felt transported to a different place, a world of beautiful things displayed on shining pedestals and gleaming glass shelves. And the shoes! To Chitra, the shoes were works of art; twisting sculptures of leather and suede, intricate criss-crossing straps and curving arches supported by impossibly high heels. Chitra had spent countless lunch breaks wandering among the displays, tracing a path through an enchanted forest of slingbacks and stilettos, breathing in the new-shoe smell like forbidden synthetic flowers blooming all around.

She harboured no illusions that any of the wonders at the Shoe Chateau would fit her overwide, ungainly feet. If a sales associate so much as looked in her direction, Chitra always made a hasty escape. How embarrassing to be caught running her fingertips from studded heel to pointed toe of a shoe she would never wear; how stupid to be seen daydreaming of delicate ankles and the caress of air on bare and uncalloused skin.

"Chitra, didja hear what I said?" In the pre-lunch lull, Chitra's mind had wandered. "Why dontcha take your fifteen now?" Fern asked, pen poised above her clipboard. She smiled knowingly. "Maybe you wanna go check out a certain store?" She waggled her eyebrows. "Maybe a certain someone who works at a certain store?"

Chitra felt her face burning to the edges of her hairnet. She knew exactly who Fern was talking about. Prakash.

He had worked at Abercrombie & Fitch as a junior sales associate before taking his rightful place as mall royalty as assistant manager at the Shoe Chateau. He was possessed of princely beauty and charm, as well as of an encyclopedic knowledge of shoes. His sexuality was a topic of heated debate among mall employees—he seemed interested in everyone and yet available to no one, his unattainability only adding to his mystique. Chitra had often heard her sisters scheming about how to catch his eye, but she had never thought to join in. Neither Prakash nor the shoes he sold were within the realm of possibility for Chitra, a fact of which she was well aware even without Gauri and Dhamini to remind her of it, which they did anyway, with relish.

Chitra made her way from the food court to the Shoe Chateau. It was busier than it should have been at this time, the news of the store closing no doubt drawing in more traffic than usual.

"Why isn't there a closing sale if you're closing?" Chitra heard a squawking voice demand. She ducked behind a circular display of sequined ballet flats and pretended to examine her own sneakered feet, hoping to escape her sisters' notice.

With the air of combined authority and indifference that all members of the upper echelon of retail staff possessed, a Shoe Chateau sales associate replied, "We're moving most stock to another Shoe Chateau. So there won't *be* a closing sale."

"Dhamini doesn't care for that," Dhamini muttered, but Gauri's self-possessed drawl drowned her out.

"Well, I heard there's going to be a special midnight sale for mall employees only," Gauri said. Her voice dropped: "A bogo."

Both Chitra and Dhamini gasped. The buy one, get one free sale was the mother of all sales, a true retail rarity and a bargain-hunters' thrill. A Shoe Chateau bogo might very well cause a riot.

The salesgirl arched a perfectly shaped eyebrow and said, "I don't know anything about that."

"Who would know?" Gauri asked, leaning forward, her eyes and nose and lips all sharp points that made the salesgirl wobble in her black ankle boots.

"Prakash might know," the salesgirl said through pursed lips painted black to match her boots. "But he's, uh, on break."

"I'm sure we can track him down," Gauri said, grabbing Dhamini's arm and dragging her away.

Chitra lowered herself onto one of the white vinyl cubes strategically placed throughout the store and allowed herself to exhale the breath she had been holding. Her toes cramped in her shoes and she reached down to poke at them ineffectually. *A bogo*, she thought. *A moonlit shopping spree.*

The chance to find not one but TWO pairs of shoes. There was something magical in the suggestion, and as Chitra reached out to stroke a sequined flat, she could almost feel her foot slipping inside it. When she closed her eyes, she saw herself dancing down the long hallway leading to the parking lot, her shoes glimmering in the red glow of the emergency-exit lights as the mall went up in flames behind her.

"Hey, are you all right? Can I get you a pair of those in your size?"

Chitra was startled out of her fantasy by a voice like cream cheese on an everything bagel — rich and smooth and soft and even. She looked up into blue eyes framed by cinnamon skin and ever-so-slightly tousled black hair. Her breath caught and she stood up too fast, dropping the flat on the floor. "Shit, sorry," she said.

Chitra and Prakash bent together to pick up the fallen shoe and his long fingers brushed hers as she released it into his hand. He grinned at her, dimples flashing. "It's fine," he said. Then, pointing the shoe at her, "You work at the food court, right?" Chitra glanced down at her uniform and Prakash laughed. "Obviously you work at the food court..." He skimmed her name tag and smiled. "...Chitra." Then with a sigh, he said, "I guess you heard we're closing."

"I heard. I'm sorry," Chitra said. The shadow of sadness that fell across his handsome face so closely mirrored what

Chitra herself felt that, for a moment, she forgot to be awestruck by him and said, "It's hard to explain why, but I'm really going to miss this place."

"Yeah," Prakash replied as he gently, lovingly, placed the glittering flat back on its display pedestal. His fingers lingered a little too long on the shoe, connected to it in a way that Chitra understood in her body and bones, and especially in her aching feet. When he pulled his hand away, Chitra saw an errant sequin stuck to the pad of his thumb, a star in his grasp in the middle of the day. Prakash's gaze fell on the lily twinkling just below the hollow of Chitra's neck. Their eyes met. "This is going to sound crazy," Prakash said, "but I have a pair of shoes you need to try on."

WITH EACH PASSING DAY, a growing current of excitement snaked from store to store, as whispers about the secret BOGO sale spread through the mall with electric speed. Only mall employees would be allowed in, only at midnight, only through the employee entrance, only with a BOGO code. Nobody who worked at the Shoe Chateau would say a word about it. Some people said it was a myth, an elaborate hoax to distract from the fact that their prices remained exorbitantly high despite their doors closing. Others devoted themselves to getting the code, the element of

exclusivity piquing the interest of even those who otherwise couldn't have cared less about shoes. Mall patrons
went about their browsing, unaware of the machinations
at play, as by bribery, trickery, seduction, or wit, the BOGO
code moved from hand to hand.

Chitra passed the time as one under a spell. She smiled
dazedly at the customers, even as the grease from their
hash brown orders splashed up from the fryer, burning her
wrists. At home, she hummed tunelessly in the kitchen,
scrubbing Gauri's tea-stained mugs and Dhamini's plates
crusty with dried spaghetti sauce, always left close to the
sink that Chitra kept full of soapy water but never in it. She
stopped craving cigarettes altogether.

"What's with you, Chitters?" Dhamini asked, dropping
her basket of laundry, pungent with her cloying perfume
and body odour combined, next to the pullout couch
where Chitra was absently braiding and unbraiding locks
of her hair. "You've been acting weird."

"Have I?" Chitra asked. She looked at her stepsister.
Despite being twins, Dhamini and Gauri could not have
been more different—Gauri stood out in every crowd,
a head taller than most, lean and eagle-eyed and quick
with cutting words; Dhamini was an average height,
with an average shape and an average voice. Without
her makeup, Dhamini's features seemed to blur together,
nondescript and unspeakably plain. A quiet kind of pity

crept into Chitra's heart as she realized how utterly forget-
table Dhamini was. At the same time, her secret sat hot
on her tongue, eager to be set free, and this combination
of knowledge and feeling made Chitra careless. "Do you
want to see something?" she asked.

From her pyjama pant pocket, Chitra withdrew a Christmas tree ornament in the shape of a glass slipper. Dhamini
peered at it, unimpressed. "What is it?"

Chitra turned the ornament over and held it up to
reveal four numbers plastered to the shoe's underside with
a label maker. "The BOGO code," she whispered.

Dhamini's eyes widened. "Dhamini needs to know how
you got that right now," she said, reaching out for the
glass shoe in Chitra's hand, but Chitra pulled it back and
dropped it into her pocket. "I can't tell you," she said. "It
was given to me in the strictest confidence."

The meanness that contorted Dhamini's face replaced
whatever pity Chitra had felt with a stabbing sense of
dread. She instantly regretted sharing Prakash's gift. But
then, that was not all he had given her. She recalled again
the feel of his sure hands rolling up her pant leg, stripping her feet of sneakers and socks, before presenting her
with a pair of floral-print pumps. He had been deaf to
her protests, easing each foot into a shoe, until her heels
had sunk snugly into the cushioned shoe beds. Chitra had
hardly dared to move, but he had pulled her up and they

had stared together at her feet, somehow made slender and soft, rising up from the garden of pink and blue and purple lilies that bloomed with every step she took. Against all odds, they were a perfect fit.

"They were made for you," Prakash had said. "You must have them."

But Chitra was already imagining what her sisters might say if they saw her wearing shoes like these, could already hear their taunts, knew they would not stand for her to have something beautiful that they did not. She shook her head. "I can't afford them," she had said. "And besides, I'm only allowed to wear flat shoes to work."

A pair of the sequined flats had been in her hand before she had time to say no. "You can have them both," he told her, before passing her a glass slipper ornament and swearing her to secrecy. "There won't be much time. The code will work for exactly one hour from midnight and you'll need to trade the glass slipper for a BOGO ticket at the Shoe Chateau doors. I'll put these on layaway for you. Will you come?"

"Yes," Chitra had said. "I'll be there."

Now the night of the sale was mere days away and the way Dhamini was looking at her made Chitra feel like a fly on the wall, aware of the spiders she lived with, uncertain which corners were snared with their webs. "Maybe..." Chitra ventured, "...maybe don't tell Gauri."

Dhamini was halfway up the basement stairs when Chitra heard her call back, "We're sisters. We share everything."

SALE DAY CAME like any other summer day, the sun rising at one end of the shining metallic sea of the mall's parking lot and setting at the other. Chitra took the bus to and from work, arriving and leaving in the dark, the glass slipper ornament always in her pocket, always within reach. She took care to prepare a proper supper for her sisters, made sure the dishes were clean, the laundry folded, and the floors swept.

Make your mother happy, her father had rasped, as blood filled his lungs and sputtered from between his lips every time he coughed. *I will, Papa*, Chitra had promised. But timid little Chitra, with her trembling mouth and wide eyes, her strange feet and soft voice, had never been enough to make her mother happy, just as her father had never been enough to satisfy her mother's expensive tastes. A man of many passions and little talent, her father had been a failed inventor, a failed musician, a failed magician, carpenter, and cook. They had never had much money while he was alive, but flowers were free to pick, so there had always been plenty of those to keep their cramped apartment fragrant and bright.

After her father breathed his last, to keep her promise, Chitra had smiled through her mother's wedding to a richer man, had been a good stepsister to his daughters, had painted herself into a perfect family that she knew made her mother happy and proud. Although her heart still grieved her father's death, at least in knowing she had kept her word, Chitra was able to find some peace, if scarce happiness, of her own. As she pulled on ill-fitting shoes and made her way from the townhouse basement to the mall food court and back each day, Chitra held on to the hope, the unspoken wish, that beyond the mall, there might be something more waiting for her. She imagined an open sky, a falling star; flowers on her feet, in her hands, in her hair; and a blue-eyed boy's arm outstretched, inviting her to dance.

As midnight drew near, Chitra donned the one dress she owned—a simple white shift she'd worn to Dhamini and Gauri's high school graduation. Neither sister had said anything about the BOGO sale and as Chitra wedged her feet into a pair of white foam flip-flops that immediately bit into the skin in the space between her toes, she allowed herself to believe they might grant her this one thing, this one night to be a girl worthy of a secret and a stunning pair of shoes.

The house was dark when Chitra crept up the basement stairs, the glass slipper ornament, her bus pass, and a little cash tucked into her mother's old purse slung over her shoulder. She paused at the hallway table, where a glass with a few wilted daisies that Chitra had plucked from the townhouse's poorly tended garden still stood. Gauri had shouted at her to throw the weeds away and Dhamini had complained they made Dhamini sneeze, but Chitra had left them there, a small act of defiance in the daisies' defence. Now, she chose the least dead daisy from the bunch, and tucked it behind her ear. She turned the door handle and breathed a sigh of relief. She could already picture Prakash's smile. And her shoes, her beautiful BOGO shoes.

All of a sudden, the lights flashed on and Chitra froze. She turned to face her stepsisters, not asleep as she had hoped, but fully dressed with hair done and makeup smeared like war paint on each one's twisted face. "Where do you think you're going all dressed up like that, Chitters?" Dhamini sneered.

Before Chitra could reply, Gauri cut in cold and smooth as ice, "You didn't think you were going to the Shoe Chateau, did you? You might have tricked Prakash into giving you that BOGO code, but we all know those shoes aren't for you."

They were advancing on her now, and she might have turned and run to the bus stop, but she knew her feet would fail her. As if reading her mind, Dhamini looked down and grimaced. "Your feet are disgusting," she hissed. She had a hand on Chitra's purse and it took only one savage tug for the worn strap to come apart, leaving the broken bag dangling in Dhamini's hand.

"My daisies!" Gauri cried, reaching out and tearing the flower from Chitra's hair. She narrowed her black-rimmed eyes and snarled, "These flowers belong to us and this house belongs to us and"—she withdrew the glass slipper from the purse Dhamini held open—"this belongs to us too."

"Please," Chitra said. "Prakash is expecting me."

Gauri cackled like a crow about to snap a rat's neck in its beak. "Oh, Chitra," she said. "What a ridiculous fantasy. You and Prakash don't make any sense. He works at the Shoe Chateau and you work at the fucking food court." She shoved her way past Chitra, dropping the crushed daisy on her way out the door.

Chitra crumpled to the floor with her head in her hands. "Face it, Chitters," Dhamini said, stepping over her. "You're a loser." She bent down to whisper, "Just like your dad."

"Take that dumb dress off," Gauri called, as she and Dhamini climbed into their father's truck. "You're not going anywhere tonight."

Chitra kicked off her shoes, curled into a ball, and wept. The hallway clock chimed midnight. She had missed the bus and all was lost. Her shoes were lost. How foolish to wish as she had wished, to hope as she had hoped. She clasped the lily at her neck and it felt, for a moment, like holding again her father's hand in hers. She closed her eyes, and in her palm, the pendant grew hot and bright, a star-shaped flower on a silver chain. She tilted her head and held the lily close to her ear. *Beyond fire there is music,* it whispered. *Beyond smoke, an open sky.* Chitra stopped her weeping and listened. *Make wishes three before the last star falls and you will dance tonight, in the flames of the mall.*

A car horn cut the silence that followed and headlights flashed on and off. Chitra walked outside to find Fern's station wagon waiting in the driveway. Fern poked her hedgehog head out the open window and hollered at Chitra, "Whatcha waiting for—a written invitation? Let's go!"

There was no time for questions. Chitra climbed in and they careened toward the mall, Fern in bathrobe and slippers, Chitra with empty hands and bare feet. The midnight sky was full of lightning, and it rumbled a warning that went widely unheeded. Chitra couldn't help but notice that the back of Fern's car was packed tight with bags and boxes. "Are you...going somewhere?" she asked.

Fern pulled into the parking lot, where they could see the crowd surrounding the employee entrance. "I thought I'd take the kids on a trip," Fern replied. The night was hot, chaos they could both feel thick in the air. Someone threw a shoe-shaped ornament at the employee door and it shattered, littering the ground with labels and glass. "A long trip." Chitra looked at her boss, but Fern was looking past her at the hulking mass of the mall and the increasingly angry mob outside it. "Good riddance," she muttered.

Chitra got out of the car and leaned down, fingers curled over the window's edge. "Thank you, Fern," Chitra said.

Fern smiled wistfully at the girl. "Didja know your dad used to come to the mall when he was out of work and had nowhere else to go?"

"You knew my father?" Chitra asked.

Fern reached over and lifted the lily Chitra wore around her neck. Her robe revealed more of her than the polo shirt of her uniform ever had and Chitra now saw that Fern's tattoos continued from her arms into the sun-spotted space of her cleavage, where a garden of faded flowers sprouted from between her breasts. She caught only a glimpse before Fern yanked her robe shut, but Chitra was almost certain that inked into the space just above her heart, Fern wore a lily to match her own. "Go get 'em, princess," Fern said, and sped away.

Chitra turned, resolute. Whatever thread of kindness or duty her father had sewn into her heart had snapped. Now she was out for blood and shoes. People were fighting for glass slippers, for space to get through the door, for reasons they would later chalk up to the fast-swirling stars and the strangeness of the night. Chitra saw Gauri's curls bobbing above the fray and headed straight for her. Just as Gauri got to the keypad to enter her stolen code, Chitra came up behind her and shouted, "Hey!"

Gauri turned and scowled. "Go home, Chitra," she said. "You don't belong here."

"Bitch, I work here," Chitra replied, then drew back her fist like it was full of stars and let it explode square against Guari's nose.

A fountain of red poured down Gauri's face as she tumbled backwards in shock. The glass slipper flew from her hand into the open Dumpster beside the door. Dhamini scrambled past Chitra to climb inside and began digging through the trash. "I'll find it, Gauri," she yelped. "Don't worry, Dhamini's got this."

Dhamini didn't notice the wriggling tails surrounding her, the red eyes, or the long yellow teeth, but Chitra knew her friends were in there, salivating, waiting for a sign. With all her strength, Chitra lifted the lid of the Dumpster, making a wall behind Dhamini as she popped up between the garbage peaks, raising the glass slipper high. Gauri's bloody hand reached out to her sister. "Give me the code!" she cried.

But Dhamini had become aware of moving things

where she stood, of maggots writhing in spoiled meat and cockroaches scuttling up her back beneath her shirt, and small furry things, warm things, hungry things, pressed against her skin. "Gauri," she whispered, "help me out."

"The code!" Gauri screamed, leaning over the Dumpster's edge, gagging at the smell. She made a swipe for the slipper, which Dhamini still held above her head.

Dhamini grabbed Gauri's flailing hand. "Come and get it," she said, and pulled her sister into the Dumpster with her. Chitra heaved the lid shut, trapping them both inside. Everyone with a glass slipper filed into the mall, so that there was no one left in the parking lot to hear their screams as the rain began to fall and the rats began to feast.

Chitra slumped against the Dumpster's side. Beside her, a small white rat missing half an ear sat up on hind legs, a glass slipper ornament with four numbers on the bottom clutched between her front paws. The rat set the ornament down next to the barefoot girl wearing the blood-spattered dress. "Thanks, Tink," Chitra said. Tinkerbell twitched her whiskers at Chitra and scurried away.

The code will only work for an hour past midnight. Chitra remembered Prakash's words, and hauled herself up, hobbling toward the employee door, her heels crunching on broken glass as she went. She turned the ornament over and punched in the code. The door buzzed and Chitra entered the mall for the last time. The scene at the Shoe Chateau was

BOGO madness — boxes strewn about, entire shelves picked clean. The midnight shoppers, the chosen few who had made it past the parking lot with their glass slippers intact, were tearing the store apart, searching for sizes, trying to carry as many shoes as possible to the cash without having their finds poached from under their very arms. They were haggling for the mirrors, the pedestals, the vinyl cubes, so that before long, there would be nothing left. Through the bars of the half-closed shutter, Chitra spied Prakash standing in the stockroom doorway, a shoebox clutched in each hand, watching wild-eyed as his beloved store was reduced to dust bunnies and discarded receipts.

Chitra staggered forward into the wall of a security guard blocking her path. Oblivious to her dishevelled appearance, he held open his hand. For a moment, Chitra's mind went blank, then she remembered — *Trade the slipper for a ticket*. She extended the glass slipper ornament. The guard glanced at it, then dropped it into a box labelled OFF SEASON — BULK full of dozens of glass slippers and offered her a BOGO ticket in return.

With ticket in hand, Chitra picked her away across what was left of the Shoe Chateau. There was a rush to get to the counter, and Chitra found herself caught in the scuffle. Someone stepped on her foot, crushing her toes, and Chitra collapsed, barely avoiding being trampled. She crawled on hands and knees toward the stockroom, toward Prakash, toward her shoes. "I'm here," she called weakly. "I made it."

"I knew you would," he said. The ground shook beneath them as Chitra clawed her way up the side of the sales counter, and hung on to it, swaying, as the fire alarm began to sound. "Give me your ticket," he said. "I'll ring you up and then..." The customers began to scream and grab whatever they could, whatever was left, as the mall sprinklers turned on, activated by the clouds of black smoke wafting past the Shoe Chateau from the direction of the food court. The security guard was nowhere to be seen, his box of glass slippers overturned and abandoned. "Let's get the fuck out of here."

Chitra placed her BOGO ticket on the counter. She lifted the lid of a shoebox and there they were—her lily-print pumps. Her perfect fit. She reached out for a shoe and then stopped. "I don't have any money," she said.

Prakash looked at her, aghast. "But... it's a BOGO."

"I know."

"You have to buy one to get one, that's how it works. You have to buy one to get any." His voice was choked, half from BOGO panic, half from smoke seeping in through the bars of the door.

"I know," Chitra said. She withdrew her hand. She had been so close. *A dream is a wish your heart makes.* She turned to go.

"Wait." Prakash pushed the shoebox toward her. "To hell with it," he said, as the ceiling started to crumble, showering them with dust. "Take them. They're yours."

Chitra put one shoe on, and then the other. They fit. Mangled toes and bloody heels and all, they still fit. "Thank you, Prakash," Chitra said, as around her neck the lily pendant went cold, its work done. Then all at once, there was a sound like an airplane descending, a deafening roar and a great rush of wind, before the final meteor crashed into the mall and everything around them went up in flames.

SOMEWHERE IN FLORIDA, an older woman reclines next to a pool. Wealth has kept her youthful and other vacationers are always surprised to discover that yes, she and her equally dashing husband have three grown daughters. She flashes pictures of her family on her phone and people are appropriately envious. *You could all be sisters,* they say. *Oh, stop!* the woman replies, flattered and proud. *But really, family is everything, isn't it?*

A news story on the television above the poolside bar catches the woman's attention. Something about meteors destroying a mall in some small town, something about two survivors, something about miracles and love.

"I still can't get a hold of the girls," her husband says, passing her a daiquiri.

On the screen, two grainy figures appear to be dancing in the rubble where the mall once stood, while firemen hose down the clusters of flame that continue to burn all around them. The woman squints to read the text at the bottom of the screen, but it is past noon and she is already a little drunk. "Does that...does that look like Chitra to you?"

The man glances at the television and chuckles. "Chitra? Dancing? You know that girl has two left feet." He lies down in the lounger next to his wife and opens a newspaper.

The woman pats her husband's knee. "I'm sure the girls are fine," she tells him, sipping her drink and stifling a yawn. She shakes her head...meteors hitting the mall. It must have happened somewhere else, somewhere far away. The woman closes her eyes and lets the fires and the girl left twirling with the flowers on her feet drift away, as if they had all been nothing more than a waking dream.

A Cure for Fear of Screaming

I never knew I was afraid to scream until the day I tried. Screaming was for those expendable girls in horror movies who are too mean, or too stupid, or too slutty to make it to the end; for bitter married couples hurling their grievances at each other across the granite islands dotting their suburban homes. But what I had told myself was contempt had been fear all along. Sometimes we let our truths rot in darkness to preserve the lies we tell in the light.

"YOU NEVER SCREAM when you come." When Veer says this to me, it's an accusation of something withheld, accompanied by a fist in my hair, a thrusting that is more violence than union. Two weeks later, we sit side by side in Dr. Cosgrove's office again, a bright and airy room on the second floor of her red-brick Victorian across from Greenwood Park. "She never screams when she comes." When Veer says this to her, it's an explanation of something observed, accompanied by folded hands, a sheepish smile conveying both confusion and regret.

"Yes, okay," she says, ever patient, voice and hair and skin like honey. "Tell me more about that. How does that make you feel?" We have been seeing Cosgrove for two years. She must know by now how many things are broken here, so maybe this seems, to her, as good a place as any to try to get a win—like treating a patient's acne, while the cancer spreads to their liver and lungs. But we both want so badly to impress, to make her proud, so we say how we feel, what we want, where we hurt, and she sends me home with instructions to practise screaming. "I understand that you may have some cultural barriers to overcome, Jhanvi. Maybe some of the shame around your body that we've talked about, hmmm? But I think you can work up to the aural expression of pleasure that Veer is looking for. Pick a safe space and try screaming on your own to start. Really dig deep, get past your outer shell. Try to find that primal part of yourself that I know is in there."

Her belief in me, in my ability to scream is intoxicating. I see her around the neighbourhood sometimes, walking her dog in the park, leaving the yoga studio with her matching mat and bag. "This is going to be good for you, Jhanvi," she says. "Learning to scream is going to help you feel so much lighter." I imagine Dr. Cosgrove lies intertwined with her husband at night, golden and sweet, the kind of woman who radiates lightness and screams with primal ease when she comes.

"Okay," I say, not wanting to let her down. "I'll try."

MY FIRST ATTEMPT, sitting cross-legged on the bedroom floor after Veer has gone to work, is a dismal failure. My scream comes out as a strangled sort of squeal that makes the cat's ears flatten as he glares at me. He has seen me come many times and has never expressed dissatisfaction, but at this pathetic display of vocal incompetence, he twitches his tail and stalks out of the room.

My second attempt, in the basement's jetted clawfooted tub, after Veer has gone to bed, is no better. (*So, it's a new tub that just looks old?* I asked Veer. *It's a character tub,* he told me. *The character elements of these homes are what elevate the East End.*) I balance the laptop on the counter's edge and play the porn we downloaded together two years ago. I mean for my scream to mimic these onscreen acrobats who do it so freely, silicone tits not quite bouncing, assholes agape. My masturbatory efforts produce a weak underwater orgasm, but when I try to scream, it's only a sad kind of keening, a sound not quite suggestive of ecstasy; something more akin to grief.

I feel obligated to make a third attempt when Veer goes down on me with Jimmy Fallon on mute, but it's less a scream and more a weird gurgling groan that makes him lift his head and ask, "What the fuck was that?"

"Nothing," I say and, start to cough. Coughing is easy. "I'm fine, don't stop."

Veer grimaces and withdraws as if the sickness has pooled in my cunt and I was about to let him drink.

I ask Veer if he wants to fuck me in the ass. This is the fourth attempt. And so he does, but even lubed and stretched, it cramps and burns and I want to scream, but all we hear is a growl, an angry guttural sound I wasn't aware that my body could make.

He pulls out too fast and asks, "What the fuck was that?"

"Nothing," I say, and start to cry. Crying is easy. "I'm fine, don't stop."

But he softens and sighs and the condom comes off and the shower goes on and I will do whatever it takes to never feel this heavy again. If there are screams inside me, they must be buried under a thousand stones, a mountain of things unsaid that I am too afraid to mine.

CONSIDER CHEMOTHERAPY. The cocktail attacks the cancerous cells and the healthy cells alike. If the patient is lucky, the healthy cells regenerate while the cancerous ones stay dead. Or if not dead, at least dormant. I dream of Dr. Cosgrove patting the back of my hand in her gentle, non-judgemental way, searching for the plumpest vein to jam the needle into.

"Are you sure this is right for me?" I ask her, anxious at the extremity of the cure.

"It's a good question," she says. "As good a place as any to begin if you're willing to do whatever it takes."

"I am!" I reply, and it's true, I am. We are Jhanvi and Veer, Veer and Jhanvi, and there is no Jhanvi without Veer. Not here in this East End life we have wanted for so long. So, for Cosgrove and for Veer, if it's a screamer they want, it's a screamer I'll be. For him, for her, for us, I'll dig out my screams, prod them loose from my ribs and belly, corral them back into my cunt where they belong, and next time Veer pins me down, I'll open my mouth and set them free.

I DECIDE THAT drastic measures are called for. I sit again cross-legged on the bedroom floor, knife in hand. This is the fifth attempt. I wait for the cat to cross my path, then scoop his lithe body into my lap and sink the knife into his furry neck. As his blood pools between my knees, I wait for the scream that now must surely come, drawn out by the horror of what I've done. But I have sacrificed so many things to be the right Jhanvi for Veer, to be light in weight and complexion alike, to heal our wounds, to fix what's torn, to make sure we belong, because we are, remember, In Love. What is this small act of violence compared to all that? Not enough. Not even close. It elicits only a toneless moan that I continue to make as I go to get the mop and bucket from the garage. The laminate is easy to clean, just as we agreed it would be when we bought the place together two years ago. Sometimes we kill in order to cure.

I return to the basement bathtub for the sixth attempt. I see now that another's pain isn't enough: *self-sacrifice* is required. I dim the lights and play the porn and beneath a cloud of berry-scented bubbles, I peel a strip of skin from my left thigh with a purple plastic razor. The pain is so much sharper than expected and I draw in my breath, eyes watering, on the edge now of the elusive scream. What comes out is a hiss, shuddering and serpentine, and even when I drag the blade, angled to wound, again over thigh, over knee, other knee, left ankle, right calf, the only screams in the room come from the computer screen where a threesome is coming to an end. When the bubbles are gone and the tinged-pink water is cold, I drain the tub and press a towel I will throw away to my bloody legs. Sometimes we hurt in order to heal.

I feel obligated to make a seventh attempt after we have gone out with friends, had drinks on a Danforth patio, strolled home hand in hand, stumbled up the stairs kissing and undressing, falling into an easy rhythm, the same sequence of positions Veer knows that I like. It fixes nothing but it feels so right. He watches my face as I come, waiting, expectant. I open my mouth to scream, but release instead an uneven stream of halting, high-pitched laughter. His jaw tightens and he finishes fast.

Afterwards, he asks, "What the fuck was so funny?"

"Nothing," I say. He has not asked about the cat or the cuts, or the pornography I left on pause, or how far I will go to keep us together, or how far gone I already am. "We should go out more. There's a new tapas place opening in the Beaches." Whatever it takes.

This is how the stones pile up, how I learn to hide in plain sight in a neighbourhood where everyone is healthy, while a cancer sleeps in the rubble of my chest.

I WANT TO say I overcame my fear of screaming, but that's not what happened. I abandoned the effort, focusing instead on finding cures for each new sickness that sprang up like weeds in the cracks between us. We brought home a cocker spaniel and, a year later, we brought home a baby boy (dogs and children being essential to the character of the East End). We talked about leaving the city and never did. We talked about getting married and never did. We saw our friends on the weekends and we saw Cosgrove every two weeks for ten more years until she died of a heart attack while on an Alaskan cruise.

Somewhere along the way, I started drinking vodka in the morning and sneaking into Veer's office at night, compulsively seeking evidence of his deceptions, of a secret life in which I had no part. Somewhere along the way, I became bitter and mean. If I could have been stupid or slutty, somewhere along the way, I could have learned to scream, but I decided long ago to be the Final Girl. The one who gets to live, but always lives in fear. It's a heavy thing, this fear, this disease, and it crushes my organs into a fine dust so that only the outer shell is left to smile and spread its legs, to say to my coworkers, "Veer and I, we are so lucky, still so In Love."

When eventually Veer dies of a cancer that will not be cured, I sit in the empty claw-footed tub, knife in hand, determined to scream at last. I begin dismantling my shell, piece by piece, wondering where I will find that primal part of myself that Cosgrove told me was somewhere here. I cut and I cut, but I cannot untangle grief and relief, and now I know, there won't be a Jhanvi after Veer.

The neighbours will claim they heard a woman screaming, but when I pry open the mouth of my shell, there is
only an outpouring of stones and I finally know what it
is to feel light. Sometimes we stay silent so that we may
survive.

Midnight at the Oasis

I used to bite the hands off my sister's Barbie dolls. I don't know why I did it; it was just a thing that happened — a slow, absent chewing in the flicker of early-morning cartoons in the basement. But then, I admit, it became something more deliberate, the hard plastic of Barbie's glued together fingers coming apart in bitter little bits between my back teeth, something satisfying in the stumps made of her slender arms.

I disfigured so many of them like that, and when Anjali would inevitably go through the laundry basket where all the dolls lived to find her latest crop of birthday presents or Christmas presents tossed back into the heap handless, she would throw such a fit. "Mummy, Adnan did it again!" Anjali would wail, carrying the evidence of my crime upstairs to show our parents.

I would be summoned from wherever I was hiding, forced to face my mother's tired disappointment and my father's terrifying rage. I think even then, at four and forty years old respectively, we both knew a mistake had been made in the configuration of my physical form. The difference was, where I would spend my life trying to correct it, he would spend his trying to deny it. He would look at the doll and look at me over his glasses and I would wait, my lip already trembling in anticipation of the punishment to come. "Why have you done this, Adnan?" he would demand. "Answer me."

"I don't know," I would mumble. "I didn't mean to."

"This is disgusting behaviour, do you hear me? Disgusting. Bring me the spoon." I would hold out my four-year-old hands and he would hit them with the back of a wooden spoon, even blows from fingers to palms to wrists, until they were red and I was blubbering. "Dolls. Are. For. Girls." Every word was punctuated with a strike. This was the real lesson. It was not the act that offended him but the interest, the mere hint of the feminine where it did not, could not, belong. "Are you a girl, Adnan?" It always came back to this. "I said, Are. You. A. Girl?" Blow by blow by blow by blow.

"No, Papa." No was the right answer.

But yes was the truth.

I loved those dolls—loved their silky hair, their sequined

dresses, their pointed toes in tiny plastic shoes. None of Anjali's friends who came to our house to play in our big basement after school seemed to mind that the dolls' hands were missing, as long as they still had all the important things to make of Barbie's life something glamorous — the hot-pink convertible, the horse, the dream house, the swimsuits, the pantsuits, the ball gowns, the various uniforms (because Barbie was a woman of many careers, after all). With all these things, we could entertain ourselves for hours, imagining new dramas and perils in which our well-dressed, women-shaped dolls could become entangled. Even handless, Barbie was beautiful. And besides, her hands were never meant to hold anything anyway. Anjali had lots of other dolls too — the kind that crawled or cried or spat up at the push of a button, but I never felt the urge to eat the hands of babies. I wasn't a monster, although the fear I inspired in my family suggested otherwise.

The last time I did it, I was six and Anjali was eight. Some auntie had given her a Holiday Barbie in a red and gold dress, layers and layers of glittering taffeta flowing out in every direction around her. Her arms didn't bend, her hands were fixed at her sides. Anjali adored her for a day, but her shining curls could not be brushed and her gold bodice could not be removed and she was quickly abandoned to the laundry basket in the basement.

I remember creeping down the stairs, retrieving her, cradling her so lovingly. More than lovingly. Longingly. Hungrily. I chewed her hands off, and when Anjali discovered her on New Year's Eve, I stood in front of my father, wet faced but, for once, defiant.

"Are you a girl, Adnan? Answer me, are you?"

My hands were already red by then, but my six-year-old brain knew what my body did not. "Yes," I told my father. "Yes, I am a girl. I just don't look like I'm supposed to."

That's when he switched from the spoon to the belt and I learned that girls like me have to be much more careful about who we give our truths to. In the wrong hands, our truths leave us covered in welts on the basement floor. Our truths make us helpless. Sometimes, they get us killed.

I was a good boy after that. I played with the right toys, wore the right clothes and gave the right answer when the question arose. If I cried and my father said, *Stop it, Adnan. What are you, a girl?* I knew to say, *No, Papa.* Lies are a necessary armour when you are a small brown girl trapped in the wrong small body.

I got out of my father's house as quickly as I could and followed my sister to the big city. I envied the relationship of sisters on TV. I wished Anjali and I could be like them— going shopping together, doing each other's hair. But that was never going to happen because Anjali didn't want a sister. Honestly, I don't think she wanted a brother either.

In the end, she had neither. The last place I expected to see her was at a bar on Church Street, leaning against a white pillar and frowning at her phone while her friends did shots around her. Two of them I recognized as friends from the old neighbourhood, girls who had sat cross-legged in our basement and walked handless Barbies back and forth across the floor, had made them kiss one overwhelmed Ken doll, specifying important details like *with or without tongue*. Except Barbie never had a tongue—her hands were merely ornamental, but her tongue was nonexistent. If her creators had given her any soft parts—a tongue, a vulva, a pair of nipples to complete the perfect symmetry of her plastic breasts, I would, almost certainly, have eaten those too.

I wasn't going to make my presence known, but Zoe recognized me and waved me over. I approached the circle. "Hi," I yelled over the music. I looked at Anjali and offered a tight-lipped smile. I had emailed her and my mother after my surgery to officially "come out," whatever that means. I sent a picture and told them my name. Neither had responded.

"Hey, Adnan! Oh shit, sorry—it's Anita now, right?"

"Oh my god, Adnan!" This from the other girl I recognized, but whose name escaped me.

Zoe jabbed Other Girl's bare midriff with her elbow. "It's *Anita*," she said. "How are you?" she asked me. "I love your hair!"

"Thanks," I said. I loved my hair too. "I'm good, still in school, working at a club here in the Village. How are you?"

Other Girl leaned in and shouted into my face, "Remember you used to do that weird thing to all the Barbie dolls' hands?" She turned to Anjali. "Remember he used to do that thing?" She grabbed one of Anjali's hands and pretended to gnaw on a finger.

Anjali snatched her hand back and glared at me. Her other friends had lost interest and were discussing where to go next.

"Did you say you work at a club?"

"What?" I had to lean down to hear what Zoe was saying. She repeated the question and I nodded. "Guys, Anjali's brother—uh, Anita—works at a club down here," she told her friends. She turned back to me. "Can you get us in for free?"

"It's not a dance club. I mean, there is dancing, but... it's a sex club."

Now I had their full attention. Where was it? What was it called? What was it like? How much did it cost? Did they have to have sex? I answered their questions. They huddled and discussed. Then one of them—the bride-to-be—threw her arms up and yelled, "I'm getting married, bitches! Let's go to the Oasis!"

There was a lot of drunken hugging and screaming. Only Anjali was not excited about this new plan. She dropped her phone into her purse and folded her arms across her chest. "I'm not going to a sex club," she said. "Those places are gross. And I'm definitely not going with my little brother, especially dressed like that. Look at him, he's fucking ridiculous."

I flinched at that. It's funny how words are so easily weaponized, harmless in some people's hands, deadly in others'. Anjali knew exactly where she was aiming hers. I had hoped to meet up here with someone who had mentioned online that they might be at the drag show, but the show had been over for half an hour and there was no sign of them. It seemed unfair to be stood up, deadnamed, and cut down by my own sister all in one night. Suddenly, I wanted all her friends to come with me to Oasis, simply out of spite. "I'm heading over there now," I said to Zoe. "You're welcome to come with me. I'll give you the grand tour!"

Out on the street, there was some half-hearted pleading with Anjali to change her mind, but it was clear my dear sister was already killing their buzz. Eventually, they put her in a cab with air kisses through the rolled-down window and promises to text the next day.

"Great to see you, sis," I told her. "Say hi to Mom and Dad for me."

"Fuck you, Adnan," she said, and the cab pulled away. I watched her go, clenching my stinging palms into fists at my sides, six years old and helpless again.

Zoe touched my shoulder. "Don't worry about her," she said.

· Other Girl linked her arm through mine. "So, Anita," she began, and I already knew from her leer what she wanted to know. "We were wondering, do you still have your..."

"Club's this way," I said, jerking her forward. There are some questions a girl should not have to answer. And some questions she should not be asked.

OASIS IS AN unassuming three-story house on a quiet side street in the Village. I checked the girls in at the front desk and took them to the locker room. "You can wear your clothes, or your underwear, or no clothes, or a towel," I explained. They were just drunk enough to brave public nudity, and soon they were all wrapped in white towels, stumbling their way to the main-floor bar. Only Zoe hesitated, leaving bra and underwear on underneath the towel that didn't quite go all the way around her. When I had known her, she had been a skinny Chinese kid who wore her hair in two long braids. Now, she wasn't skinny anymore and she had traded her pigtails for a pixie cut with bangs that swept across her forehead.

I set them up with drinks and left them to watch the pole-dancing competition on the dance floor. In the staff change room, I put on my uniform—black shorts, sneakers, and a bright blue crop top with the Oasis logo across the front. By the time I made it back to the bar, I was not entirely surprised to find Other Girl (unsuccessfully) trying to climb the pole. "Let me take you on a tour," I said, pulling her away, prompting the others to follow.

Along with the dance floor, the hot tub and the heated outdoor pool were the main features of the club at ground level. On the second floor, I pointed out the dungeon, filled with dark wood and black vinyl furniture pieces designed for kinky fun, and across the hall, the ballroom, an elegant, open space painted a rich purple and lined with plush seating, all facing a low platform stage with a demonstration bed in the middle.

On the third floor, we found an empty table near the bar and I gathered them 'round. "You can explore on your own up here," I said. "There are a bunch of different rooms where couples or groups can have sex. Always ask before you watch or play, and if you play, play safe." I pointed to the jars of condoms at the bar. "Any questions?"

"What exactly do you do here?" Zoe asked.

"Bartend, clean, refill condoms, wash towels, give tours—whatever needs to be done, really," I said. I put a hand on her bare shoulder and leaned in. "You don't have to stay if it's not your scene." Her hair smelled like coconut. "I have to go to work, but I'll find you later, okay?"

She nodded and I left. Those lube dispensers don't fill themselves.

I lost track of them over the course of the night and it was nearly three in the morning when I saw Zoe again, making out with a woman on a couch beside the bar. I saw them head for the locker room together, and when the lights came on, they were dressed, leaving hand in hand. Zoe stopped at the bar to say goodbye. "It was really great to see you, Anita," she said. "Thanks for bringing us here. It wasn't like I thought it would be."

I laughed. "Yeah, people think it will be super shady, or dirty, or weird—like some creepy *Eyes Wide Shut* shit. But"—I gestured at the people filing out behind her, younger and older, every shape, size, and colour, people laughing and kissing, a microcosm of the city behind the sex club doors—"that's not what it is at all."

She nodded and then—I don't know how else to describe it—we had a moment. We looked at each other and there was a spark in the air between us. But her new friend was waiting and I had to close up and we let the moment slip away.

"Bye, Anita," she said.

"Bye, Zoe."

She turned to leave, but then turned back. "Hey, in case I don't see you again, I just want to say, I'm glad you're . . . *you*, finally."

I looked at the woman waiting for Zoe by the door and grinned. "I'm glad you're you too," I said. Then she was gone.

When I got home to my apartment, I rummaged through my closet until I found the small grey bin, one of the only things I took with me when I left home. Opening it felt like opening a coffin, like I was disturbing something dead, but I opened it anyway and looked at the Barbies piled up inside. The clothes they were wearing were faded and out of style, but otherwise, they hadn't aged a day. I picked them up, one by one, the feel of them so familiar in my aching hands. They were so beautiful to me still, with their long legs and blond hair and full breasts. I didn't need to look for these things in a bin, I could find them in the mirror when I went to look at myself. Why wasn't it enough?

I held up Holiday Barbie and ran my thumbs over the jagged stumps where her hands were missing. "Why did I do this to you?" I asked her. Her blue eyes were unblinking, her smile fixed, and I suppose that is as close to forgiveness as one can hope for from a doll. I put the Barbies back in the bin and put the bin away. I didn't think about them again for a long time. I went to bed as the sun was coming up and dreamt of pink cars and pixie cuts and hands on my body that knew the right questions to ask of each part of me they encountered. And when to be still and ask for nothing more.

———

I DIDN'T EXPECT to run into Zoe again, but she turned up at Oasis the next weekend, and the next, and the next, sometimes with a woman, sometimes on her own. When it was slow, she sat at the bar, towel wrapped around her waist, and we talked. I discovered that I found her funny and weird and cute and kind and, eventually, I asked her if she'd like to see me outside of the club.

"Like, go on a date?" she asked.

I laughed because it seemed like such an old-fashioned thing to do, but I replied, "Yeah, like go on a date. With me. Is that something you'd be interested in?"

It was and we did and she became my girlfriend, although we still saw other people, when our bodies made such requests. She taught me how to make dumplings and I taught her all my bhangra moves. We got a place together and spent two years cooking and dancing and talking and fucking, and I decided that I would only invite into my life people who made me think, laugh, or come. Two out of three at least.

When Zoe and I decided to get married, we both reached out to Anjali—she was my sister and one of Zoe's oldest friends, and it felt important to both of us that she be there. She didn't return our calls, only replied to one of Zoe's texts to say, *I can't.*

No explanation, no apology, no attempt at an excuse. Just, *I can't.*

It hurt me more than I wanted to admit.

In the kitchen, Zoe said, "It can't have been easy for her, growing up in your house either. I'm sure deep down she loves you, in her own way."

"What does that mean?" I asked. *In her own way.* My mother had said the same thing when I lay bruised and broken on the basement floor. *Papa only wants what's best for you,* beta. *He loves you, in his own way.*

I didn't know what to do with that kind of love. I still don't.

My sister wasn't there for my wedding. She wasn't there when Zoe and I became foster parents to two-year-old Celeste, and she wasn't there when we officially adopted Celeste two years after that. Sometimes, I still think about the irony of me becoming a wife and mother, building my own little family, while Anjali is out there somewhere, on her own. It should have been satisfying, but instead, it made me sad.

In my life with Zoe and Celeste and the friends who held us in their circles of care and the club that served as a second home, there wasn't much to remind me of my sister. Until one day, close to Christmas, I came home to find a heap of handless reminders strewn across the kitchen table, unearthed from the depths of the closet and the past.

"Look what I found, Mama Nita!" Celeste cried, holding up a Barbie doll in each hand. How could it take so little to break me, to take me right back to that basement floor? Celeste did not understand my sudden tears or my anger or my demand that they all go right back in the bin they came from. Zoe said I was being unreasonable, I said she was being unfair, and when we told Celeste to go to her room, she said we were both being *so mean.*

In the morning, we pulled out the bin and looked at the Barbies together. "You know, when I was a little girl, I wanted to look like this more than anything," Zoe said, stroking a doll's hair. "I thought people would like me better with blond hair and blue eyes, or at least that I'd be prettier."

"But you are pretty, Mama Zoe," Celeste told her so earnestly, I thought my heart might break. My sweet wife. I hadn't considered that she too had wished to be something other than what she was. She had wished to be beautiful. I had wished to be whole. Celeste looked up at us and asked, "What happened to their hands?"

Zoe and I glanced at each other across the kitchen table. I shrugged. "I ate them."

Celeste giggled. "Oh, Mama Nita," she said, "you're so weird." She examined the stumps, then her own hands. Then she said, "Let's make new hands."

"New hands..." I repeated. It was doable with a little

clay and paint. "They won't look exactly right," I warned.

Celeste held up Holiday Barbie. "She needs gold hands," she said. "Or alien hands. Or"—her eyes went wide—"... glitter hands!"

"Don't you have an art degree?" Zoe teased. "Clearly, this is what it's all been for."

And she was right, in more ways than one.

We spent the week between Christmas and New Year's making new hands. Celeste had none of the reverence for the dolls that had so afflicted Zoe and me, and they ended up with slightly misshapen, multicoloured hands that stuck out at odd angles. Celeste adored them though, and they became scattered among the books and blocks, the cars, dolls, and crayons that never seemed to find their way off the floor. They were just part of the regular mess of things, sparkling and strange and whole at last.

NEW YEAR'S EVE is the busiest night of the year at Oasis. I work because they need the help and the money is good. And because I need to keep busy, on this day more than other days, to keep memory from hardening into new pain, and the club remains, for me, a safe and fertile space. Zoe says New Year's Eve is overrated and I know she'll be asleep before the ball drops. She knows I need to be at the club and I am grateful for the knowing. This too is love.

The party is mermaid-themed and the space is packed. In the glow of blue lights, we count down from ten, and as midnight strikes, I kiss my lover across the bar. We sip champagne from plastic flutes and they tell me I am beautiful before kissing each of my palms and going upstairs to fuck their partners. This too is love.

On the first day of a new year, I slip into bed next to my wife and find our daughter curled up beside her. Celeste wakes momentarily as I shift her small body over and she smiles, touching the mermaid paint still staining my skin. I stroke her coconut-sweet hair and her eyes close. I would do anything for you, my soft, fierce girl, asleep with a cheek against the back of my hand. This too is love.

Somewhere in the city, the family into whose hands I was born mourns the boy I never was, fails to see who I am, who I've always been. The failure is theirs, not mine, and I am strong enough to let them go, to speak of my body with gentle words, to make of myself a woman who is sparkling and strange and whole. There is space for all these things. This too, after all, is love.

Chrysalis

Radhika sat alone in the grass, soaking up the sunlight. It was surprisingly warm for late autumn in Montreal. She tilted her face toward the light, toward the blanket of delphinium-blue sky above, and listened to the wind whispering seductively to the swaying trees, undressing them leaf by leaf. A bitterness rose in her throat, like bile but less solid. The remnants of something rotten swallowed long ago. She turned a hard stare on the stone in front of her. Grey slate. The cheapest stone in the catalogue. *You have no right*, Radhika thought, but she couldn't decide if the sentiment was meant for the graveyard, which had no right to be so soft and bright and beautiful around her, or for her mother, who had no right to be dead.

Radhika glanced at the adjacent stone. Coral-coloured marble flecked with gold. Only the best for one Mme. Marie

Beauchamp, Cherished Wife and Loving Mother. A fresh bouquet of sunflowers, left perhaps by Marie's well-loved children, sat propped against the stone, obscuring a portion of her lengthy epitaph. Radhika wondered if the dead receive flowers the way the living do, if leaving them at one's grave was akin to leaving them at one's cubicle to draw the curious gaze of passing coworkers. She felt her mother seething in the afterlife somewhere, consumed with envy over her neighbour-in-death's expensive tombstone and aggressively cheerful adornments. Then she was there in the sunlight—not in cancer-riddled body, but in voice; close and clear and indignant.

Look, Kaka! That grave has this thing, how can we say... This kind of ... curb appeal!

Radhika rolled her eyes at the stone. "Please, sunflowers are so tacky, Ma."

What's tacky? I know what I like!

"I should have just had you cremated."

What nonsense! This is a perfectly good spot. You can fix it up, nah? Then you and Michael can bring all your babies to visit me here.

The warmth of the mother in her mind was as real as the warmth of the autumn sun. Radhika could almost feel her mother's plump, vaccination-scarred arm pulling her off the ground and propelling her forward, but there was no arm there to link with hers, not anymore. Radhika inhaled, seeking the familiar scent of Yardley English Rose talcum powder dusted on forehead, nose, and neck (and discreetly in between thighs, in the cleft between the breasts). But neither the grave nor the grass nor the trees nor the grief held at bay by the series of bad decisions that had brought her to this place smelled like anything she knew. There was nothing left that smelled like home.

An old car, sputtering on borrowed time, pulled up between the rows of graves and idled on the paved pathway. Radhika didn't move. She wondered if she might turn to stone herself eventually, vampire-like, if she let the sun penetrate her skin for long enough. Someone would have to drink her blood for that to happen. Someone would have to help her transform. She stood and looked down at the two gravestones side by side — her mother's and Mme. Beauchamp's. She wondered if as she transformed from woman to monster to stone, she might be offered a choice between marble or slate.

Milo handed her a cup of coffee as she climbed into the car. "Are you going to do this every time?" he asked.

Radhika shrugged. Digging in her jacket pocket, she fished out her wedding ring and forced it back onto her finger. "I don't know yet," she said.

RADHIKA SAT ALONE on the train, caught in a shaft of sunlight. The train had become her backwards cocoon. From the moment she entered Gare Centrale, her wings, her eyes, her legs all slowly began to close, until she emerged five hours and twenty-two minutes later, a ground creeper once again, slinking through Union Station, descending into the tunnels shooting out into the night.

The attendant came by with his cart on wheels. "Something to drink, miss? *Quelque chose à boire?*"

Radhika gave him a smile. *"Oui, merci,"* she replied, the words exaggerated in her anglophone accent. She wanted them to be suggestive, indecent, wanted every second while she was between two bodies, two worlds in which she could not exist at once, to drip with decisions that could go either way. She ordered a coffee and rummaged through her bag for the three dollars she owed.

Her bag was full of stupid things. Old receipts for purchases she couldn't return, makeup she never wore, restaurant mints that had come with the bill, a broken change purse, and a lot of loose change. Her mother suddenly there on the train beside her, voice incredulous. *Three dollars for a cup of coffee, Kaka? Must be such a rich girl now!*

The train lurched and Radhika tossed her hair, willing the attendant to see her, to spill hot coffee into her lap, to return her smile, to press her back into the window and sink his teeth into her neck. He poured the coffee with practised ease, setting the cardboard cup on her tray without spilling a drop. His gaze on her was expectant, devoid of desire. Radhika found two loonies and four quarters and dropped the fistful of metal into his open palm. *What kind of creature do you see sitting here?* she wanted to ask him. *Centipede, stone, or bat?* But she only sipped her coffee in silence, and he pushed the cart away.

BACK IN TORONTO, Michael cooked an Instant Pot dinner and talked about an article he had read in the *Star*, a friend he ran into at the gym, a construction notice he saw posted in the elevator. Radhika checked her email on her phone and read a blog post on her laptop, about the ten hottest hair trends for fall. They ate, and they watched half a hockey game and half a movie starring young Tom Hanks.

Radhika got a text from Milo. *What are you doing right now?*

Nothing. Thinking about you.

When are you coming back?

Radhika said, "I just got an email from my boss. They need me back in Montreal."

Michael yawned. "It's weird they put you on this account, you don't even speak French."

"My résumé says I speak French."

"Who wrote your résumé?"

"I did."

"I hate to break it to you, babe, but just because you wrote it doesn't make it true."

Later that night, Michael slipped into her from behind, quietly, almost apologetically. It was not unpleasant. In the light from the hall, she watched the big hand move on the clock, past the four, then the five. He finished midway through the six. He kissed the back of her neck, reached around and curled his fingers between her pressed-together legs. He knew how to do it, it wouldn't take long to get her there. She closed her eyes and let it happen. It was these small acts of generosity that made her feel the worst.

RADHIKA SAT ALONE on a pile of leaves, warmed by the sunlight. The wind was past the stage of wooing now, stripping the trees of their remaining finery with an efficient violence until their branches were bare. In the car, Radhika's coffee was getting cold. She wished she knew the appropriate amount of time to spend at a grave. Too little felt callous, disrespectful to the dead; too much felt morose and melodramatic, a pantomime of grief.

There was a flower shop in the train station, Fleuriste

Centre-Ville, where she had remembered to buy a bouquet of flowers this time. When she asked the man behind the counter if he had *"fleurs du soleil,"* he had stared at her blankly. Either he didn't have the right flowers or she didn't have the right words. She had left instead with a cheap bunch of carnations, some gerberas, and greenery in between.

Radhika laid the flowers down in front of her mother's gravestone, then reconsidered and set them upright, mirroring Mme. Beauchamp's now-withered sunflowers. Her hands were getting cold and she jammed them into her jacket pockets, finding a crumpled receipt in one, her wedding ring in the other. Her mother's voice in her ear, in her head, in her bones — approving of the flowers, disapproving of everything else. *What are you doing here, Kaka? You know better than this, don't you? Smarten up!* Maybe a pinched earlobe. A light slap on the cheek to give her rebuke an extra sting.

The car circled around and Radhika pushed herself to her feet, brushing the leaves that clung to her tights from the backs of her legs. Milo offered her coffee cup as she got in, and she took it, enclosed it with both hands, and left the ring in her pocket.

"Are you okay?" he asked. Radhika looked at his face and it was like staring too long at stars or smoke, his features constantly in flux. He was all flannel and frayed edges and fangs, monstrous and beautiful, blurry in the graveyard's tree-filtered light.

"I don't know yet," she said.

RADHIKA SPRAWLED ALONE on the bed, bathed in afternoon sunlight. She could hear Milo on his phone in the bathroom, his French too fast for her to understand. He brought both phone and freshly rolled joint back to the bed, where he stretched out beside her. He inhaled deeply and blew the warm smoke into the space between her breasts. Radhika imagined roses blooming there, her skin the dark soil, his breath the seed.

They fucked all over his shabby Plateau apartment. The bed was for smoking, for snacking, maybe for sleeping. The hallway, the shower, the kitchen table, bent over an armchair that the cat had torn apart, up against the living room wall — those were the places they did it. Whether they came together violently or tenderly, either way, the sounds never mattered to anyone. The neighbours screamed at each other in French and Portuguese. A dog barked listlessly and a man with a guitar stood on the corner and strummed a barely discernible "Bird on the Wire." They went together to X-Tasy Video on Ste-Catherine and picked up piles of sex trash: strawberry-flavoured condoms and plastic handcuffs covered in synthetic purple fur, DVDs with obscene covers that were $7.99 each, or three for $20.00. They bought wedges of soft cheese, greasy chips, and dark chocolate and ate the way they fucked—ravenously, unselfconsciously, ferociously.

When there was no sunlight left, Radhika put herself back together and stuck her head out the second-floor window, searching the street below for vacant cabs. No Ubers, no hotels, no restaurants offering mints with the bill. Nothing on credit cards, she reasoned. Nothing on paper. Nothing real.

"There's two on the corner," she said.

"Do you want me to come with you?" Milo asked.

"No," Radhika replied. Her cocoon only had room for one.

"Stay," Milo said. "Stay the night."

"I can't," Radhika told him. "I'll miss my train." But he was already unzipping her dress, encircling her, unravelling her, and she was melting into him again. If anyone on the street had looked up, they would have seen a woman's naked back framed by an open window, radiating heat, rippling with pleasure, arched in release. But nobody was looking. Montreal was a city of monsters making strange music in the shadow of a mountain.

RADHIKA SAT ALONE on the balcony in a shrinking pool of sunlight. The view was desolate. Grey skies merged with grey water, colliding randomly with concrete and glass. *Spectacular Lakefront Living in the Heart of the City!* a banner across an abandoned building on the other side of the street proclaimed. There was construction everywhere. Every day something old came down and something new went up. Way, way up. Her mother's wrinkled nose and pursed lips as she had demanded, *What is this condo-mondo nonsense, Kaka? You can't have babies here!*

Radhika's mother and Toronto were long-time enemies, although they had never spent more than a week-end together. When Radhika thought of the patchwork of her childhood, following her father from contract to contract at one university after another — McGill, Queen's, Western, Dalhousie — it had seemed odd that Toronto had never curled its greasy fingers in invitation; Toronto with its new money and its old money and its whirlpool-like pull if you wanted your work to matter, if you wanted your name in the mouths of all the right people. It was only later, after her father was dead, that Radhika understood that Toronto had beckoned many times over the years, opening side doors and back doors and trap doors all over the city, but her mother had always refused the call. When Radhika asked her mother about it, she had simply replied that it wasn't the kind of place she could ever call home.

Radhika had moved to Toronto partly out of spite and partly because she hoped the city would transform her into who she was meant to be. Michael was a native son, descended from a long line of Bay Street bankers and Lake Muskoka boaters. He had hair like wheat and features that remained constant in any light. He might have been born in khakis and a collared shirt. There was a logic to the love that he offered, a safety in his ready smile, a simplicity in the life she had chosen by choosing him. Michael radiated sweetness and ease because it was all he had ever known. His parents' cloying sympathy at her mother's funeral had made Radhika wish for talons or serrated teeth, so that she might tear them both apart, limb from impeccably dressed limb.

Radhika and Michael lived on the forty-ninth floor, in a sleekly designed box filled with gleaming steel and granite. Their tower was attached to the tower next to it via skyway tunnel and connected to an underground parking lot, which connected to an underground shopping mall, which connected, eventually, to a subway entrance. Squinting down at the traffic, then up at the sun, it dawned on Radhika that this was not a place for winged creatures. There were so many intersecting corridors through the sky and through the earth that there was neither room nor reason to fly.

"What are you doing out here?" Michael asked her, poking his head through the balcony's sliding door.

"I think they're finally going to tear that building down," Radhika said.

"It's practically winter," Michael replied. "It's too late to build anything now."

By the time Radhika realized she was pregnant, both banner and building were gone, leaving a gaping hole in the ground.

RADHIKA CURLED UP alone in the armchair, as the apartment filled with sunlight. She picked stuffing from the chair's shredded arms and watched Milo sleep as the street below began opening its eyes and its doors to the coral-coloured sky, singing to the mountain as the first buses rumbled past. From the floor, the disjointed frames of a poolside orgy played out on Milo's computer screen, the DVD skipping painfully in the overheated machine. *Baise-moi, ba-a-a-ise-moi-oi-ah.*

She should leave before he woke, leave a note, fish a lipstick from the bottom of her bag and leave the imprint of her lips on all the windows, across the cracks in the walls. When eventually Milo stirred, she was still there, waiting. There was a wildness in him that she wanted to absorb through his skin and the black ink of his eyes. His particular brand of poison was an intoxicating glimpse at other people she could be, other stories she could tell, other lives that were not hers, not yet. He squinted at her, then at his phone. There were no clocks here.

"Did you know I was born in Montreal?" Radhika asked him.

"So was I," he said, crawling off the bed so that he was on his knees, spreading her legs apart.

"Do you think it's weird I was born here but I don't speak French?"

"Your résumé says you speak French."

"But I wrote my own résumé."

"Then it must be true."

He buried his head between her thighs, his stubble prickly, like the sting of so many perverse bees. It was a sensation that used to make her squirm, but now, after being so thoroughly fingered and tongued, stretched and skewered, she sat perfectly still except for the clenching of her fists and the curling of her toes. She let the pleasure uncoil slowly, slithering up into her bones, infiltrating her blood. He dragged her onto the floor and fucked her, descending on her with a wet mouth, bitter and sticky, pumping honey and venom into her veins.

"I think I'd like to be buried here," she told him.

"Jesus, it's too early for this," he said. He turned the computer off on his way to the kitchen and Radhika couldn't tell if he meant the conversation or the porn or both. She didn't look or feel any different, it was only the knowledge of difference that was heavy.

RADHIKA SLID THE door shut, blocking out the sunlight. The bathroom on the train was so small she could barely turn around without bumping into something and the constant motion combined with the pain threw her off balance. The lighting was fluorescent, tinted green. The smell of stale urine and industrial soap made her nauseous but there was nowhere else to go, nowhere else for this thing to happen.

"Are you okay, miss? *Ça va bien?*" The first time the attendant asked the question from the other side of the door, his voice was breezy, more of a warning than anything else. *You better not be smoking in there*, it said. The second time, it was more anxious, edged with annoyance. She had to get back in her seat. She had been in there too long.

"I'm not feeling very well," Radhika answered. She thought of her mother's oversized purse, how it used to be full of useful things: Kleenex, Band-Aids, Aspirins, maxi-pads, safety pins, perfume samples in little vials, nail clippers, pens, and always a notebook (always full of notes). The toilet seat was wet, her thighs were wet, the floor was wet. Roses blooming everywhere. Her mother's voice saying, *My beautiful girl. My smart, smart girl. How did you get yourself into this mess?*

Radhika heard the announcement over the intercom: "Ladies and gentlemen, Toronto will be our next stop and final destination. We will be arriving at Union Station in approximately ten minutes. *Mesdames et messieurs...*" She tuned it out, rocking back and forth, breathing through the wrenching in her belly and trying not to make a mess in the midst of a messy situation. She let it happen. Maybe because it was what she wanted, or maybe because she had no choice.

RADHIKA SAT ON the sofa, sobbing in the weak winter sunlight.

"You've been acting so strangely. Just tell me what's going on," Michael said.

If there was ever a time to come clean about everything, it would be now. *I hate to break it to you, babe... I hate to break you... I hate you...*

"I lost the baby," Radhika said.

Michael wrapped his freckled arms around her, murmured, "I didn't even know," and "It's not your fault," and "We can try again if that's what you want." Radhika rested her cheek against the embroidered horseman with mallet raised high on Michael's shirt. She imagined her baby coming into the world between two cities, its heart stopping, its freshly fused cells breaking apart along the train tracks. No wings, no eyes, no name, no home. Not even a person yet, she reasoned. Not real. Not anymore.

RADHIKA CROUCHED IN the snow, blinded by the sunlight. The trees were stoic, survivors of a seduction-turned-rape. In the absence of the wind, they turned their accusing eyes on her. She had nothing to bury. I should have kept the blood, she thought. Instead of just flushing it away, like shit, like cocaine in a movie, like nothing at all.

A black SUV pulled up and a mother, a father, and a child spilled out. The father lit a cigarette and leaned against the car door, smoking and watching the child pack snow into uneven balls with mittened hands. The mother carried a bouquet of sunflowers and made her way to Mme. Beauchamp. She smiled politely at Radhika, but said nothing. There was no protocol for graveside small talk.

The child threw a snowball in their direction and it grazed Radhika's shoulder. *"Allons-y, maman,"* he called to her, impatient, bored with death.

"Ah, je m'excuse," the mother said, shaking her head as if to say *You know how kids are.* We women, we mothers, we know. She left the flowers, rested a hand on the marble for

a moment, and then returned to her family who returned to their car and were gone.

Radhika pulled her frozen hands from her pockets and dug a shallow grave in the snow. There was no car, no coffee, no cocoon waiting for her now. There was only a bag, now empty of makeup, mints, and money, empty of receipts, empty of broken things. It contained inside a pen and a notebook; a series of hopes hastily written, waiting to be true. She buried her wedding ring in the hole she had made and walked away, eyes open, wings beating furiously against the bitter cold.

Acknowledgements

My heartfelt thanks to everyone who helped bring this book into the world.

To my editor, Shivaun Hearne, and the entire team at House of Anansi — thank you for seeing something sparkling and strange and whole in these stories.

Thank you to all the editors at various literary magazines and anthologies who published my work in earlier forms, and to all the readers of and subscribers to independent literary magazines and journals. Your support of these necessary platforms for short fiction makes all the difference.

Thank you to Farzana Doctor for providing early mentorship and being the first to say, "So there might be a book here." And to Jaclyn Desforges, around whose kitchen table many of these stories began.

Thank you to my instructors at the University of Toronto School of Continuing Studies Creative Writing Program, for your generous feedback and encouragement. Your (virtual) classrooms were where many of these stories were finished.

Thank you as well to Zarmina Rafi, Stephen Thomas, Colleen Fisher-Tully, Terri Coles, Alicia Freeborn, Lisa Gasson-Gardner, and Jennifer Thompson for being first readers and endless cheerleaders.

I am grateful to the Ontario Arts Council for generous support in writing this book.

I want to thank my mother, Rose Varghese, for supporting my education (despite misgivings about the usefulness of an English degree) and for giving me the roots and wings that have allowed me to pursue a creative life.

Finally, to my partner, Jeff Geady — I could not have done any of this without you. Your love and support and patience and humour sustain me and my pen. Thank you for everything.

© Jesse Valvasori

ANUJA VARGHESE is a writer and editor whose work has appeared in *Hobart*, the *Malahat Review*, the *Fiddlehead*, *Plenitude Magazine*, and others. Her stories have been recognized in the PRISM International Short Fiction Contest and the Alice Munro Festival Short Story Competition and nominated for the Pushcart Prize. She lives in Hamilton, Ontario. *Chrysalis* is her first book.

anujavarghese.com